Cocky Veteran

By Tiffani Lynn

Editor: Hourglass Editing

Proofreading by – Finley Proofreading & Katie MacGregor

Cover Design by – Wicked Smart Designs

❀ Created with Vellum

CONTENTS

INTRODUCTION

Cocky Veteran is a standalone story inspired by Vi Keeland and Penelope Ward's Cocky Bastard. It's published as part of the Cocky Hero Club world, a series of original works, written by various authors, and inspired by Keeland and Ward's *New York Times* bestselling series.

This book is dedicated to my own cocky veteran. I love you, Teddy.

1

FERRIS

The punk rock music pulsing through my headphones feeds my soul as I work on my Trigonometry homework while seated at the scratched up, old, wooden dining room table. The music is the only thing that brings me solace these days. The last two years have been a special kind of hell, and if it weren't for the words in these songs I would've been completely alone. Most of these punk bands seem to get the pain of the human condition without being the slow, sappy emo type shit. The driving bass and pounding drums keep me from wallowing in the bottom of the black pit. It's the music of the struggling masses that still have the will to live, and it's the only thing keeping me going.

Thank God I'm good at math and don't have to concentrate too much to come up with the right answers because this house is always chaotic. Everything that's wrong with the foster care system can be found in this particular home. Fighting, filth, abuse, out of control kids, and useless foster careers. I only have four more years of places like this, and

I'll blaze out of here so fast people will wonder if I even existed.

The thump of feet pounding on the floorboards shakes the room of this rickety old place. I glance up to see who's about to run in here. Ezra and Jermaine blow through the room but not before smacking me upside the head as they go by. Those two are punks, and they're always taking shots at me and the other kids who aren't as big as they are. Of course, they do it when the adults are nowhere to be found. Those little assholes act like angels when the case workers visit or adults of any kind are within hearing distance, brown nosing, and making me want to gag. I hate them.

No, that's not right.

That's not a strong enough emotion.

I completely loathe them to my core.

To me, those two are everything that's ugly and dark in the world rolled into two teenage size punks. All of us stuck in this place have it bad already, but to have to live with the dickhead duo on top of it just makes it a living hell. If it weren't for them, I could deal with this place better than I do now. They're also the reason I don't sleep much. If you sleep with them in the house, it's likely you'll get beat up, or your hair shaved, or your eyebrows removed. I've even heard whispers of one of them grabbing guys' junk while they sleep. Not cool.

Life sucks, big time.

It's hard to go to school when you're scrawny, nerdy, and excel at math and science. But add being a damn orphan and you become a pariah. It seems the smart kids would hang out with me since we're in all the same classes and like the same things, but nope, their parents won't allow it. One dude's mom even referred to me as riff raff as she whispered to another mom. Not quietly though, obviously, since I heard it loud and clear. The kid turned his wide eyes to me, knowing she was being too loud, and his pink cheeks gave his embarrassment away. After that I just stayed away from him so he didn't have to deal with a pissed off mother. Do I wish I had friends to help me get through this? Yes, but the truth is, as long as I have my music and am left alone by the dickhead duo, I can keep going.

TWO MONTHS LATER...

MY LEGS ARE STRETCHED out in front of me on the rickety railing along the front porch as I lounge in the old rocking chair in the Florida sunshine. The consuming heat has taken over, and although the humidity is high, I don't mind roasting like this if it means I can sit away from everyone and listen to my music in peace. I've managed to lay low for at least two hours. I'm silently counting the number of sweat streams running from my neck into the collar of my shirt when Ezra pushes through the door followed by Jermaine and a new addition to the dickhead duo, Luke. They could be the terrible trio now but honestly, they're dumb enough to share a brain, so in my mind I have continued calling them the dickhead duo as my own private fuck you to them. I keep my eyes down hoping to stay off their radar. I knew this little bit of peace was too good to be true, and luck is never on my side.

"You trying to burst into flames like your daddy?" Ezra jokes in a wicked tone that has me on the defensive immediately. Jermaine and Luke chuckle uncomfortably and glance at each other. Because the foster mom at this house has loose lips, everyone here knows my family died in a house

fire that I escaped because I was spending the night at a
friend's house. Most of the kids here would never bring it up
in front of me. They might whisper about it behind my
back. These three live by their own rules. Nothing is off
limits, including the worst days of my life. I keep my eyes on
the floor like I can't hear them, even though I can hear every
word they toss at me like grenades. "Wonder if your mommy
liked burnt dick?" Talk of my mom grabs my attention, and
my eyes narrow and turn to him. Even when they were alive,
I didn't like people talking about my mom. I loathe mama
jokes. My dad taught us to respect and love our mother, so
talk of her pushes my detonate button like nothing else. I
grit my teeth and hold still because I can feel the rage
coming on.

"That's what I thought. Pussy! You're a pussy. Bet if your
mommy wasn't charcoal she'd dress you up like your sister
and put pretty bows in that stringy ass hair of yours." Now
they all crack up like it's the funniest thing they've ever
heard. My chest tightens with overwhelming, blistering
anger. My fingertips tingle as my blood pressure jumps. I
rise to my feet and tuck my Walkman in my pocket and
glare at them. That sets them off further.

"Ohhh, Ferris doesn't like me calling him a pussy. Poor,
sad, pussy Ferris, no family, and no one who gives a shit.
Even the foster parents don't give a shit about you. Sucks to
be you." They turn to leave, laughing and joking about me
being a pussy, when Ezra pauses and turns back to say, "No
need to get bent out of shape about your mom, she was a
white trash piece of shit anyway. I heard the fire was her
fault. She was probably trying to kill you so she didn't have
to raise a pussy boy, but was so dumb she burned the rest of
'em up too."

They move down the steps, howling with laughter,

when the tension running through my body snaps, sending me into a blind rage, I dive after Ezra first. We tumble to the ground in a heap. Fists are flying, we're kicking and clawing and wrestling. Everything I've buried inside, every emotion I've been hiding, everything I've been feeling for the past several years has burned inside me long enough, and I'm taking it out on Ezra. It takes the other two a little longer to jump in. I was doing good with the element of surprise and the out-of-control anger I'm unleashing, until the others jump in. I'm not able to hold them off for long, and as soon as they are able, they double me over with kicks to my face, ribs, and stomach. I try to keep fighting. It's the last several kicks when I feel the cracks in my ribs. One of them grabs my arm and wrenches it behind my back. The bolt of lightning that shoots through my shoulder and down my arm is so painful I scream. The last thing I remember is someone's shoe heading for my face before it all goes black.

Later that evening, I'm lying on a hospital bed in the emergency room. My body hurts all over. The social worker is seated in a chair beside the bed, trying to get me to talk about the fight. Of course, those assholes told her I started it, that I charged them for no reason. The foster parents believe the dickhead duo, but by the way the social worker is looking at me and the questions she's asking, I'm not so sure she does. Though, I learned a long time ago you don't rat anyone out, no matter what happens. You'll pay for it somehow if you do. And I think I've paid enough for five lifetimes already, I'm not making it worse. Which is why I'm sitting here silently while my eyes continue to swell and I turn away from her.

"We have no choice but to remove you from that home since you won't tell me what happened. I realize that's your seventh home since your parents died, but I can't take you back there if you might put other kids in danger."

Oh, what bullshit. It's so absurd I can't help myself, and I cough out an ugly laugh. Of course, she feels like I'm putting other kids in danger, did she not notice it was three to one? Whatever. They'll go after another kid, and the truth will come out. Or so I hope.

"What aren't you telling me?" she inquires softly, almost begging me to tell her.

I swallow hard as I focus on the closed curtain pulled around us and keep my mouth clamped shut.

"Fine, I've got a call into another home. You'll be in here for a few days. With your face all busted up, the dislocated shoulder, broken arm, and broken ribs, you'll require more care than the other kids this couple has taken in the past, so we'll see if they can even handle it. I'll be back in a few minutes, and hopefully we'll have something figured out. Do you have any questions?"

"Did someone get my Walkman?" I ask the only important question.

"It got crushed in the fight. Sorry." Although her words say sorry, her tone says she doesn't give a crap. Her lack of concern for me losing the only thing that keeps me going doesn't give me any incentive to say anything else to her.

That's the thing that finally breaks me, losing the Walkman. Angry, hot tears fill my eyes and slide down my face as she leaves. It was my only saving grace in this hell I call my life. My music. How will I survive the next place without that? I can't even begin to think of what shithole they'll offload me into next.

They operated the next day but I had a nasty reaction to penicillin and some internal bleeding that no one noticed until I almost died. Now it's almost two weeks later when they finally tell me I can go home. Only they don't understand that I don't have a home. Maybe in theory they get it, but not in reality, and I've decided it almost physically hurts to even hear the word 'home'. The doctor was late making rounds and even later putting in orders, not to mention there was a shift change for the nurses, so I sat in the room waiting all day almost expecting them to keep me one more day since it was so late. But they've finally given my social worker my discharge instructions, and she's walking quietly alongside me as the nurse's aide pushes me in a wheelchair to the entrance. I'm quiet and nervous. I haven't fully recovered from the last foster home hell and am not ready to go through anything like that again. I hate not knowing what I'm walking into.

Once I settle into the front seat of her four-door sedan with my body aching a little—but not as badly as it did a few days ago—she pulls out of the parking lot and heads in the opposite direction of the last foster home. About fifteen minutes later, we're pulling into an orderly upper middle class neighborhood with clean yards and expensive landscaping. There are no couches or broken recliners on front porches, or dogs chained to trees in the front yards. I've never been in a foster home like this. Most of them have been rundown and smaller than they should be for the number of kids they take in. Even the home I lived in with my family was a step down from this. I mean my family home was neat, clean and an appropriate size for all the people living there, but this is almost next level. Pools in every back yard, perfect landscaping at each house and little decorative flags in most of the yards welcoming guests.

When we pull into the driveway, I glance at the clock to see it's nine o'clock at night. The social worker turns to me. "These are good people. They weren't ready to add anyone to the house, but they did because I told them about your physical state. They're doing us a favor so don't screw this up."

I nod once to let her know I get it, but inside I sizzle with anger. It's ridiculous I got blamed for everything that happened with the dickhead duo. I mean seriously, even if I didn't rat them out, it was THREE on ONE! That should make what happened obvious. Those assholes played very convincing victims, and I not only got a long hospital stay I also got a lecture and probably some crappy stuff written about me in my file.

The social worker gets out of the car as a man and woman step out of the house and stop on the porch. The man is tall and handsome with a full head of brown hair and a blank expression on his face. The woman is probably a foot shorter than the man and is pretty in the same well-kept way my mom was with her straight, blonde, shoulder-length hair shining in the light from the porch lamp. She looks like a mom you'd find on a television sitcom. Both are dressed in T-shirts and shorts. The man wraps his arm around her shoulders and holds her close as they both watch the social worker open my door for me. I can't open the door on my own yet since my right shoulder and right arm are the ones that were injured and both are still sore.

I step out of the car feeling a sense of calm I haven't felt in a long time. I have no idea why other than the house looks clean and the people look more like my own parents than any of the other foster parents so far. When the car door closes and the social worker steps around me so they can fully see me, an audible gasp emanates from the woman and the man's lips purse. I pause a moment, wondering if they'll turn me away with the way I look. My heart begins to thump hard in my chest.

The woman speaks first and steps out of her husband's embrace. "Chloe, oh my God."

She steps close to me, and I stop and stare at her, unsure of what to do. Is she horrified by me? My bruises have started to fade, but that hasn't helped me look any better. It will probably take another week or two. When the woman slowly reaches for my brow that has several stitches in it, I watch warily and chant in my head: *Don't send me back, don't send me back, don't send me back.*

"Oh honey. What did they do to you?" Her eyes search my face as they glisten with unshed tears.

"Ferris, meet Mr. and Mrs. Pearsal." Mrs. Pearsal turns to Chloe and shoos her with her hand. "Oh, please. It's Audrey and Ray. Mr. and Mrs. Pearsal are my in-laws." Her smile is soft as she turns back to me. "Did they give you anything for pain at the hospital?" I shake my head, not ready to speak. "Are you hungry?" I nod. "Okay, Ray can take you in and get you something to eat and something for the pain. I'll be there in a minute. I need to get some paperwork from Chloe."

I nod once and turn my attention to Ray. He ushers me inside the front door, through the entryway that opens up to a great room, angling me toward the kitchen section. "Do you have any clothes to change into?" he asks as he flips the lights on in the enormous kitchen space. I'm wearing the clothes I was wearing the day I went to the hospital. The staff was nice enough to wash them for me, but they're still torn and ragged after the fight. I shake my head and focus back on the kitchen. The dining table is big enough to fit an army. Everything is painted in white and light gray. It all looks so clean. On the fridge are pictures colored by what seems to be little kids and schoolwork with big letter A's and B's on them.

My head drops, and my eyes shift to the floor. I'm pulled back in time to my parents' house. Our fridge was the same way. Our artwork, good grades, and awards covered the fridge with colorful magnets. That ache I get in the middle of my chest when I think about my family comes back strong. I miss them so much.

Ray's voice pulls me back to the moment. "Okay, Pax and Ben's clothes will be too big, but you might be able to wear Ren's. Tomorrow we'll get you some clothes of your own. All right let's get you fed. Audrey makes a killer roast, and we have carrots and potatoes I can warm up too. Will that work?"

I nod and whisper. "Thank you."

He stops spooning the stuff on the plate and looks up at me. "Son, you're safe here. You treat us with respect, and we'll do the same. If you need anything, please let us know."

I nod slightly again. This guy is going to think I'm an idiot, but I just don't have much to say that means anything right now. Maybe tomorrow I will, but for now I'm a little intimidated and a lot afraid of getting sent to another place. What if I say something offensive or appalling? I don't want to mess this up.

A couple minutes later, the front door closes with a small thump and Audrey joins Ray by the microwave. She kisses his cheek and gives him a simple but sweet smile. I haven't witnessed that kind of affection in a long time. "I can see Ray has the food situation under control so I'm going to the bathroom to find some Motrin. Chloe gave me your discharge papers, and I think if we alternate Motrin and Tylenol it'll help you with the remainder of the pain. I'll also grab you a change of clothes from Renaldo's room."

"I told him we would get him some clothes of his own

tomorrow. Do you have time or do you want me to take off work?"

She smiles brightly at me. "I have plenty of time. The only thing on the agenda is Renaldo's speech therapy at four o'clock, so that gives us the whole day to take care of things and get you enrolled at the high school. You'll meet Renaldo, Ben, Courtney, and Paxton tomorrow. Ben, Renaldo, and Paxton all go to your school so you'll know some people when you get there. Even though school started last week, I don't think we'll send you until next week when your face heals up. No need to start a new school looking like you went a couple rounds with Manny Pacquiao."

I breathe a sigh of relief because although I've had to go to a bunch of different schools over the years I never had to start looking like this. It's hard enough being the new kid. If you show up as the new kid and it's obvious you've been beat up you're just asking for trouble. There's always some dude who will think it's a challenge to beat you down more. No thanks.

Within an hour I've eaten, wiped down with a washcloth, brushed my teeth with a toothbrush they gave me and am wearing a pair of baggy basketball shorts and a T-shirt that come close enough to fitting. Once I come out of the bathroom, Audrey and Ray call me into their spacious but somehow still cozy living room and gesture for me to take a seat on the grey leather sectional. They're seated across from me and next to each other.

Ray speaks first. "I know you've had a long day, but we need to go over a few things with you so you understand how things work around here. You're expected to go to school every day, do your homework, turn it in on time, and eventually get involved in some kind of extracurricular activity. That can be anything you find interesting, and we can discuss that after you get adjusted a little. You'll clean up after yourself, and next week your name will go on the chore chart so you'll be expected to do your chore for the week. Everyone has to do it. It's important you treat everyone in the house with respect. No fighting. If there is an issue that would bring you to blows, you need to come see me. If I'm not home, text me. In this house, we face everything together, and we never turn on each other. We're a unit. We know it'll take time for you to feel that, but eventually you will. However, we do know there are a lot of us in the house, seven to be exact, and at times we can annoy each other so I try to get in front of any issues ahead of time.

"There is only one girl in the house, Courtney. She's off limits for dating. From here on out she's like your sister, and you will treat her accordingly. We also want you to know we have an open-door policy. You can come to us about anything, and we will try to help you any way we can. We don't allow drugs in the house, and you can't drink until you are of legal age." Ray takes a breath and relaxes back into the chair like he's relieved that part is over. "Now, what we'd like to know is what you would like from us?"

I stare at them, wondering if what he just said is real, or if it's all for show. Can a house like this be real? Is everyone who lives here a robot, or do they just hide their shit like the dickhead duo? I'm not sure what to say. When I don't respond Ray fills the quiet.

"Okay, I know it's going to take time to get used to all of this. By the sound of it, you didn't come from a place even remotely like this. How about I tell you what I can think of and you let me know if any questions come up." He holds up a finger. "First, you can expect to sleep easy here. None of the kids in this house will ever physically hurt you. No one will steal your stuff. You'll get three meals a day, and most of them are good. Sometimes when Ben cooks it's questionable, but otherwise the food is good."

Audrey giggles and smacks his arm playfully. "Be nice," she admonishes him.

He tilts his head and raises an eyebrow in a comical kind of way. "When you taste it you'll know what I'm talking about. You will survive it but barely."

Audrey rolls her eyes and smiles. "He's only kidding. What we're trying to tell you is that we want you to feel like this is home; we want you to be comfortable. We know from the other kids that life in some of the other homes is rough. We don't want that here. No lying, no stealing, no cheating, and no fighting. Respect is key. If you can live with that then you can call this home."

I nod a few times so they know I understand. Deep down hope blossoms, but it all seems unreal after everything I've been through. When I meet the other kids tomorrow I'm sure this perfect little bubble will burst.

"Okay, well, we know it's been a long day, and I have to work early tomorrow. How about we show you where you're sleeping. You'll share a room with Paxton. You guys are the same age, and he's an easy-going guy."

"Thank you," I whisper, afraid if I speak any louder this will all be a dream, and I'll wake up.

Ray and Audrey lead me up the stairs and down a hallway lined with pictures of kids at different ages. They stop at the second room on the left, and Audrey quietly opens the door. There is a creak from the bed and a light comes on. "Oh, hi, honey. I'm sorry I was trying to be quiet."

A voice much more masculine than mine replies, "No problem, Ma. I was still awake." I peek beyond Audrey to get a good view of a clean room that could house any normal teenage boy anywhere in the United States. Audrey and Ray peel away from the door and gesture for me to go in. My heart is pounding. The not knowing what you are getting into, and who you are sharing a room with is the most nerve wracking thing ever. A new roommate could mean anything. Asshole, adult brown noser who is nice in front of adults and an asshole when they are out of earshot, emo dude, silent and scary, or the hardest to find...cool—which I've never gotten.

I'm sure Paxton can hear my heart thudding against my rib cage as I take in the two extra-long twin beds along opposite walls, both covered with navy blue bedding that is much nicer than anything I've had since I've been in foster care. My eyes flick up to take in the couple of posters of sports superstars that line the wall above the bed Paxton is laying in. There are two nightstands, one by each bed with small lamps and digital clocks on each one, and for some reason this settles my nerves a little. Don't ask me why. I've never paid attention to nightstands in my life. Until now when I realize this is the first time I will have one to put my book on when I'm done reading at night. Stupid I know, but that little thing feels good at this moment of uncertainty. In a surprise move, Paxton sits up and swings his legs over to rest on the floor.

"Hey, man. I'm Pax." Great, this guy is clearly a jock. He has muscles most kids our age don't have and tanned skin. This is the kind of dude all the girls in school fall in love with instantly. There couldn't be a guy more my opposite if I conjured him myself. Damn. Guys like him are known to stuff guys like me in garbage cans and knock books out of our arms in the hallways at school. How bad will it be sharing a room with him?

"Ferris," I return quietly, nervous again. My stomach

twists. I was praying for a good night's sleep, but that's not going to happen with this guy in the bed next to me.

Pax studies me for a minute, but not in a hostile way, more of an assessing way. Audrey and Ray stand awkwardly by the door looking back and forth between us. "It's okay, Mom. We're cool. I'll take care of him." Pax says before turning to me. "Are you going to school tomorrow?"

I shake my head.

"Okay. Well I'll be quiet getting ready for school. We can hang out when I get home from football practice. I'll have some homework, but I'll make time. Get some rest. If you need anything just wake me up."

"I'll be okay," I respond quietly as I sit on the edge of the bed.

"If the look of you right now says anything, it lets me know you'll be okay here. Nothing you've been through before you walked through those doors will touch you here. You're safe, and I'll make sure of it."

There is no way I can believe what he's saying. The smoldering pile of ashes my home became and the array of crappy foster homes I've lived in make that almost impossible.

Audrey's face gets soft as she looks between us. She shuffles over to Pax and kisses his head tenderly. My heart aches a little remembering the feeling of my mother's comfort. Ray follows suit. Audrey pauses in front of me and brushes some of my stringy blonde hair out of my face with gentle fingers. "Goodnight, sweetie. Let Pax know if you need anything at all. He can come get us if he needs to."

"Night, sport," he says to Pax and then turns to me. "Night, bud." Then they turn off the light and leave the room, closing the door behind them.

I fold the covers back and climb in, laying on my back

and looking up at the ceiling. Pax's deep voice is quiet as he reminds me, "It's going to be okay. You'll like my brothers and sister. Life is different here, promise."

I stay quiet because I don't believe those kinds of fairy-tales anymore, but I'm not one to pick fights with dudes twice my size.

2

TONI

Thirteen Years Later.

My reflection in the bathroom mirror is a good indicator of how rough this past year has been. My hair resembles something the squirrels create to raise their babies in, and the bags under my eyes could hold all the clothes I'd likely need for a two-week vacation in Bermuda. Not that I'll be going on a trip to Bermuda anytime soon, or ever again actually, but that's not the point. What it is, is not pretty.

"Hey! Hey! Help me! Help me! I need to get out of here!" my father's loud, frightened voice carries down the small hallway, and I'm reminded why I look the way I do. I hurry out of the room and down the little hallway of our duplex to find him reaching up toward the ceiling as he calls for help. He's not hurt, and no one is around, but it's still a heart-breaking sight for me. One I see all too often these days.

"Dad!" I say a little sharper than I mean to. "Dad, it's okay. You're safe. I'm here, taking care of you. This is our home. I just went to the bathroom."

Close to a minute passes as he studies my face, looks

around the room, then comes back to my face, our eyes meeting again. It's as if the fog in his brain clears and thank God it's quickly this time. His face brightens with a smile. "Ah, my sweet Toni. Always my good girl. I knew you'd save me. Where are we?"

I sigh, pressing gently on his arms so he'll lower them, and then lean over to kiss his forehead. "We're in Crystal River, Florida." I sigh and kiss his cheek. "It doesn't matter where we are though. You know I'll always take care of you, Dad. Are you hungry? Ready for some breakfast?" I ask even though it's closer to lunch than breakfast.

"Donuts! I want donuts!" he shouts out gleefully like a child waiting for a Saturday morning treat.

"Are you sure, Dad? I ask, knowing good and well he wants donuts. He hasn't eaten anything for breakfast except Little Debbie mini powdered donuts for the last two years. In fact, his meals are the exact same every day. When I try to incorporate other foods, he refuses to eat. Everything I read, and I read a lot, indicates that routine and familiarity help lessen the confusion for a dementia patient. So I do my best to keep our lives as consistent as possible for him, including serving him the same things every day, even if it means I hunt through three grocery stores to make sure he has exactly what he wants.

Once breakfast is complete, I lead him to the recliner and help him get seated with old episodes of Gunsmoke playing on the television. He won't move for the next couple of hours, which gives me time to do laundry, take a shower, and pull myself together for work.

At 3:45, Mrs. Gonzalez, who we call Gigi, arrives and greets my father with a kiss on his cheek and a warm smile. She's older than him by five or six years, making her about sixty-seven or sixty-eight. Gigi is youthful with quite a bit of energy and a sunny disposition. She's his evening caregiver while I work. He thinks she's his girlfriend, and she goes along with it because he doesn't make any sexual advances toward her.

Someone from my support group yelled at me about deceiving him, which made me feel like a jerk. After I talked to Gigi about it though, she explained that it's not hurting anyone. If it gives him comfort, and he's not being inappropriate, it shouldn't matter what other people think. It makes him happy and lord knows he deserves all the goodness he can get. I'm so thankful for Gigi's help. I pay her for it, but she doesn't have to be as kind or accommodating as she is. I know that for a fact because the woman who fills in when Gigi takes a day off or goes on vacation is a do-your-job-and-go-home kind of caregiver. Gigi infuses love and happiness into everything she does in my home.

"Chica, take your time tonight. Have a glass of wine after work. Relax. You don't need to rush home. You know he'll already be in bed, and you deserve a little breathing room."

"Thanks, Gigi, but by that time of the night I'm exhausted. If I get off early for some reason, I'll take you up on that. Call me if anything comes up—"

She holds up her hand to stop me. "I know, you're right down the road. Don't worry. He's okay. It's going to be a good night." She stands, follows me to the door, and smiles as she shuts it behind me. I hear the lock click and breathe a sigh of relief. I feel guilty thinking that my time at work is an escape, but that's exactly what it is. I love my dad and don't mind taking care of him, but I had no idea how consuming it would be until it became my everyday life.

I drive the short distance to the Lobster Lounge and swing into a spot behind the building where the employees are expected to park. Then I grab my apron and my purse and walk inside. The first one to greet me is Stacey. She's been working here longer than me and stays because she really likes it. Her husband, Hudson, makes great money as a hot shot security specialist for a local security company. Her last marriage was as bad as mine, in an abusive kind of way, and she said she'll never be financially dependent on anyone again, so she keeps working. I admire that about her, and I'm super thankful too because we get along great, and she's the closest thing I have to a friend here. She would probably be a real friend I do things with if I had time. Instead, I work and take care of my dad. I have learned over time to be thankful that I have a work friend, and I leave it at that.

As I slide the time card into the clock and hear the punch of the time stamp on the paper Stacey comes up beside me and rests her hip against the desk. "I just got here a few minutes ago. Sounds like they had a busy lunch shift and are expecting it to be busy tonight too. Apparently, the Crystal River Rotary is coming in tonight, and we will still be open to the public."

"That will make the night go by fast." I flash her a quick smile. Hard work is not a problem for me. I like it when it's busy, the time passes faster, and the tips are usually better.

"Yeah, but Hudson's out of town, and the baby will be asleep, so I'll be bored when I get home. I hate when he's gone. My house is too quiet."

"You're so full of it. There's no way your house is quiet with those crazy dogs running around, even if your baby is asleep," I remind her about her adorable and rambunctious French Bulldogs, Nitro and Remington, who have more energy than any animal I've ever seen. Those dogs keep them on their toes.

"I know you're right, but it's different without Hudson at home. I know he's quiet and all, but it's just different."

"I wish I could say I know what you're talking about, but I don't. My ex-husband was such a bastard the last couple years we were together I was happy when he had to be out of town. I miss having someone to go home to besides my dad, but I'm glad it's not him."

Stacey sighs and casts her eyes to the ground. "I'm sorry. That was insensitive as hell."

"Nah, if I were you I'd be sad that Hudson's gone too. That man is too hot for his own good." I wink at her, but before we can finish our conversation Nick, the bartender, leans around the corner. "Hey lovely ladies," he croons in that ridiculously flirty way he has. "I just sat two families, one in each of your sections."

"Where is Heather? Isn't that her job?"

"Yeah, but she's out sick so we're all on hostess duty tonight."

Stacey and I groan simultaneously. I love my job but hate hostess duty. My first two months on the job here were as a hostess. It was the only job I could find in this town that I was qualified for. Thank goodness Lola, one of their long-time servers left, and they gave me the opportunity to train as a server, or I would've pulled my hair out by now.

Two hours into our shift, a family of five is seated at the only open table in the place, which is my section. When I reach them, I pull out my note pad from my apron, grab the pen stuck behind my ear, and smile. I recognize them right away because they're in here quite a bit, but they're friends of Stacey and always sit in her section. I imagine that's what they were hoping for tonight, but there weren't any available seats. The man is smoking hot. Tall, dark hair, thick with muscles, and a grin that will melt your panties off at twenty-five yards. He's movie quality hot. However, he's so obviously in love with his gorgeous auburn-haired wife he wouldn't think about another woman's panties. When they come in, he's always finding some small way to touch her, and they constantly smile at each other like lovesick fools. If it wasn't so cute I'd probably gag at the sweetness factor. They have their adorable curly-haired little girl and a cute, older, mixed son that they adopted. Stacey talks about them quite a bit, but we've never been introduced. "Hey guys! I can get you started with drinks if you want, and then I can see if Stacey can take your table."

"That's cool, but it's busy, and this is your section. We don't mind having you take care of us. You're Toni, right?" the man inquires.

"Yeah, I am. Are you sure?"

His wife finally smiles softly at me, and her gaze shifts to their son. "Yes, of course it's okay. Don't you think so, Linc?" She asks the boy. He grins, turns away, and nods his head.

"Don't be shy. It's okay to smile at the pretty lady and talk to her," the dad says.

"Dad," he groans, and the dad laughs.

"I'm Paxton, and this is my wife, Shay, my son Lincoln, and our daughter Morgan." I give them a goofy wave, and before I can ask what they'd like to drink, another guy, this one tall with black framed glasses and a boyish grin, joins the table, taking the last seat. "Sorry I'm late. That interview went longer than I expected," the man explains. He's thinner with lighter skin and hair than Paxton. The hair on top of his head is a little longer and carelessly styled while the sides are super short. His light eyes are a cross between green and blue. He grabs the menu, and the motion pulls my attention to his forearms, which are veined and strong like he lifts weight or heavy equipment. They are not in keeping with the skinny nerd thing he has going on. "Oh good, right in time for introductions. This is my brother Ferris."

My mouth opens before my brain has a chance to stop it. "Your brother?" my tone is way more disbelieving than is polite.

"See, dude? You shouldn't even introduce me to anyone that way because no one believes us." He laughs a little.

Paxton straightens in his chair and raises an eyebrow at me as if to say, why are you so rude?

Under that kind of scrutiny, I fidget. "I'm sorry, I didn't mean anything by it. I just..." I trail off because I don't know how to get out of this. I should have just sent Stacey over here.

"No biggie," Ferris says, brushing it off. "Pax is my foster brother. We don't look alike because we aren't related, but it doesn't make him any less handsome, so don't hold it against him." Ferris winks at me and resumes looking at the menu with a silly smirk on his face. I bet that's a practiced line. If they were foster brothers, then they grew up together and Ferris probably got that a lot. I'm still embarrassed by how rude I was and wish I could melt into the floorboards.

"Ferris." Paxton's serious tone gets Ferris' attention.

"Relax, big brother, everything is cool. What's everyone having?"

Shay reaches over and pats Paxton's leg, probably telling him to let it go. "I could use a beer," Ferris speaks up first. "What about you, Linc?"

His cheeks turn pink, and he tips his face down to look at the table. "Root beer, please," he mumbles.

"Linc, make eye contact and speak up," Pax insists. You can tell the poor kid is mortified, but he does what he's told.

"Do you want one of our new curly straws? We just got

them in." I grin at him, and he blushes again and nods. When he glances at his dad, his dad tilts his head and gives him what can only be described as a fatherly look and Lincoln continues, "Yes please." Shay orders a Coke for herself, a cup of milk for Morgan, and Paxton orders a water.

"Okay, I'll be right back." I hurry away, checking on two tables on my way to get their drink order. When I reach the bar to get Ferris's beer, Nick looks at me and then back toward the dining room. "You know them?"

"Nah, they're friends of Stacey's. They said it was okay for me to keep their table tonight."

"Why are they looking at you?"

"What?" I ask as I turn to see what he's talking about. Sure enough, everyone at the table is staring at me. They all go back to their conversation and my cheeks heat again. "I said something rude without thinking." If I didn't just embarrass myself I would assume my family screwed their family or their friends over in the business-gone-bad debacle. My ex-husband Lenny got my dad and I in a hellish situation and his shit has infected my life in the worst ways.

The more I think about my encounter with them the more familiar I realize Pax's face is, not just from his visits here to the Lobster Lounge. I may forget a name, in fact I do that often, but it's rare I forget a face. By the time the drinks are loaded on my tray and up on my shoulder I'm certain I know him from somewhere. When I approach the table, Pax is kicked back with his arm stretched out to rub his wife's shoulder, his legs are spread lazily in that way hot guys sit sometimes. It's at this moment that the epiphany hits and I get a couple of flashes of memories from my high school cafeteria and one of my gymnasium. I think we went to high school together. Though, the boy in my memory is smaller and less developed than the man in front of me, but it's certainly the same person. I don't think we were in the same graduating class, but I'm positive we went to the same high school. Of course, Paxton's bigger and obviously badder than he was in high school, but Ferris doesn't look familiar at all. They're brothers though, so it would make sense Ferris went to my school too. Maybe he's much younger than we are. I keep sifting through memories, and Ferris just doesn't stand out.

Realization hits. If they knew me in high school, recognized me now and live anywhere close, I'm sure they've seen my name and face on the news. With all that was printed about my family, if they figure it out they'll want to change their minds and have Stacey take their table. I've become a serious pariah to a lot of people in Ocala. It's why I brought my dad almost an hour away to Crystal River. Ocala is far enough away that we won't run into people often, but close enough that we are available to the district attorney prosecuting the case. It just wasn't safe for us to stay in that town while Lenny's trial is going on, and my pride couldn't take any more grocery store or gas station confrontations from dad's former employees.

Ocala Transport Corp—the trucking company my father owned and ran for thirty years—got busted for drug trafficking thanks to my ex-husband, Lenny. While my dad was in police custody after the bust, his lawyer realized he had dementia. He had him diagnosed by a doctor, while the prosecutor required a second opinion. Even though it's been proven my dad didn't understand what was going on, none of his employees believe it. They still blame him. The one they should be blaming is me. I was so busy avoiding Lenny, I avoided the office and consequently didn't see my dad enough, didn't notice his cognitive decline. I should have been around, and I should have seen it coming on. It was easier for me to spend my time on our ranch caring for and riding the horses than face reality.

I was so damn selfish. I've never expected dementia to start so early. In my mind, dementia happens to eighty-year-olds. Not my sixty-year-old father. If I never would've married a lying, manipulating, piece of shit like Lenny, maybe none of this would have happened. Now we're paying for it. Paying for my naiveté and my need to hide when things get tough instead of facing them head on.

Everyone is quiet as I pass out the drinks. A quick glance around the room to try to locate Stacey comes up fruitless, so I proceed with caution by tucking the tray under my arm and pulling my notepad back out. I'm sure they can hear the tremble in my voice when I ask, "Are you ready to order?"

Shay's smile is warm as she nods and clears her throat. "I am. Let's start with the kids."

Once I've taken their orders, I scurry toward the kitchen before they can change their minds and demand Stacey take over for me. No one has been rude to me or given me dirty looks, but it seems like they might recognize me and want to ask me about it. Confrontation is not my thing, and I've had more of it than I care to remember this past year, so I keep their drinks filled and my time at their table to a minimum.

When they pay their bill and exit the building, I breathe a sigh of relief. I haven't run into anyone who recognizes me or my dad since coming to Crystal River, but we aren't that far from Ocala, so I know it's bound to happen at some point. But I'll do anything to delay that day.

3

FERRIS

The coffee cup in my hand has a few more swallows of the lukewarm liquid left in it, but my attention is on the vibrant yellow and orange sunflowers planted along the fence outside the kitchen window. Staying with my brother, Paxton, and his family has been amazing. I love his property, his home, and most of all the company of him, his wife, Shay, his 12-year-old adopted son, Lincoln, and his one-year-old daughter, Morgan. Paxton lived on this piece of property where their house sits, but left when the state removed him from his biological parents' care. When his biological grandfather died, he willed the property to Pax. Shay grew up on the property next door, and the two of them used to run through these fields together. When Pax returned to claim the property, he was reunited with Shay and a different kind of friendship formed between them. Now they're raising their growing family on this land and loving every minute. I can see why. It's a version of heaven for sure, just hotter than all get out. Florida is like that though, hot all year 'round.

"Bro, are you even listening?" Pax snaps me out of my thoughts with his deep voice.

"What? I'm sorry I was zoned out." I shrug and grin at him.

"Quit tuning me out. Are you ready to leave? Mike's waiting for us."

I take one last drink of my coffee and move to the sink to wash my cup. "Yup. I've been ready. It was you who took forever to get to the kitchen. I was waiting for twenty minutes."

"Bullshit. You only got out here ten minutes ahead of me. I saw the light pop on when I was getting dressed." He shakes his head at me. "You're just jealous my morning was spent in the company of a beautiful redhead and yours was with a rosy palm."

At that exact moment, the beautiful redhead he's refer-ring to glides through the door into the kitchen and smacks him on the arm. "Paxton Pearsall! That was rude!" Her cheeks are pink, probably from embarrassment, but Pax doesn't seem to care. He smiles at her and pulls her into his arms for a hard and fast kiss. "Sorry, sweetheart. Listen, we need to get going before all the scallopers hit the river and ruin our fishing. We'll meet you and the kids at the Lobster Lounge at noon for lunch. Stacey is reserving us a table."

She continues to glare, but I can tell it's all for show at this point. "Behave."

He laughs, kisses her again, and strides out of the kitchen with all his loose-limbed grace. My brother has had that quiet confidence since the day we met. It's a trait I've envied in him for years. Now I just accept that's who he is and not something I'll ever have. I'm not one of those guys who gets jealous of stuff like that or wishes I was someone else. At least not anymore. I'm comfortable in my own skin even if I know I'm a little awkward at times. Accepting my nerdy qualities and embracing them took years, but I finally accomplished it.

"See you later, Shay." I flash her a small smile as I peek back around the corner at her.

"Bye, Ferris. Don't let him bully you. If he comes back with a black-eye, I'll know it's his fault."

It's my turn to laugh as I call out, "Sure thing!" It's funny she says this because although I'm a far cry from the scrawny teenager that moved into Paxton's room seventeen years ago, he's still bigger than me by a lot. Not to mention his skills as a Navy SEAL are certain to make him a formidable opponent. But above all, Paxton and I have never physically fought. We may have bickered a little when we were younger, but he's always more likely to be my protector than my foe.

Pax wasn't lying when he said he'd take care of me that first night when I moved to the Pearsall home. He has always kept to that promise like it's his job in life. Even going as far as to fight Dennis, his best friend, when he caught the guy kicking my ass after school one afternoon. Dennis never liked me or the fact that Pax spent so much time with me. This made me Dennis's favorite secret punching bag. I refused to say anything to anyone about what was going on with Dennis because I was afraid they would remove me from the Pearsall home. Paxton suspected something was going on with me, he just wasn't sure what. When Pax walked up on Dennis treating me to his daily dose of crap, Pax taught Dennis a lesson he didn't quickly forget. The P.E. coach is the one who broke it up. Pax was suspended for three days and Dennis for ten since I came clean and explained to the principal that I had been getting bullied and beaten up for a few weeks. I hated being a rat, but I wasn't going to let Pax go down for defending me. He was pissed at me for not telling him what was going on with his so-called friend, but he got over it quickly. Pax and I grew closer, and Dennis became persona non-grata with Pax.

Pax and I didn't run in the same crowd in school. He was popular, athletic, and adored by students and staff alike. I hung out with the emo/rocker crowd. You know the kids clothed all in black who express their love for rock and punk music with colored hair, black nails, and band T-shirts. They were good friends to me during my high school years, but very different from Pax's crowd. So Pax and I hung out outside of school. Although he never ignored me, even going out of his way to introduce me around and help me out in the beginning. The day I moved into the Pearsall house was the second-best day of my life, preceded only by the last barbecue I had with my biological family.

We pull up to Mike Wade's house situated in a beautiful lot right on Crystal River. He's Paxton's boss and friend and the husband of Summer Arden Wade, the gorgeous actress almost every man I know would give his eye teeth to be with. Lucky bastard. She's as sweet as she is beautiful and I end up blushing most of the time I'm in her presence like Linc did with Toni the waitress at the Lobster Lounge. It's embarrassing as hell. I met them right after Pax took the job at Sunset Security, and we get along great. I make it a point to see them whenever I visit.

As my feet clear the grass and step up on the creaky dock, Scooter, Mike's basset hound, who is hanging out on the dock watching Mike load a cooler on the boat, slowly trots his long round body over to us like the little old man he is. Pax reaches down to pet him first and then moves on. I squat down and give him a good rub down, causing him to flip on his back and expose his belly to me.

"How you doin' today, buddy? I see you haven't backed off the treats since I saw you last. I guess at your age it would be cruel to put you on a diet." He eyes me as I continue to scratch his belly, a doggie groan escaping as I hit his favorite spot. When I stand, Summer is standing at the back door holding the hand of her four-year-old replica with the same curly blonde hair and light complexion, Sarah.

"Good morning, ladies," I greet them, beating back the starstruck feeling that sets in when I see her.

"Morning, Ferris. You going to lunch with us after fishing?"

"Yeah, I try to never miss a trip to the Lobster Lounge."

"Good! We can catch up then. It's good to see you. I know your brother is happy to have you home."

"Me too. After the last couple years in Wyoming, freezing my butt off, I'm glad to be out here sweating and enjoying the humidity."

"I bet. I shot a movie in Montana a couple years ago and about froze to death." She leans over a little and looks at Sarah. "You can go down and give daddy a hug and kiss, but don't get on the boat. This fishing trip is only for the boys, okay?" Her little face scrunches up in frustration. "Why can't one girl go?"

"Because there are times when it's just boy time. Now is one of those times. Daddy will take you fishing tomorrow."

Sarah stomps her foot and glares at her mother for a long time. Summer never backs down. This must be a common thing between the two because neither moves nor breaks eye contact. I would probably burst out laughing if my daughter gave me that stubborn glare complete with pouting bottom lip. "Fine," Sarah finally relents.

Summer's eyebrow rises. "How about you say 'Yes, ma'am' to me?"

Sarah grumbles a 'yes ma'am' and then stomps down the dock to her dad.

"Our daughter hasn't quite learned to share her dad or their fishing time."

"I don't blame her. Fishing is fun, especially with her dad."

Summer flashes me her dazzling smile, and I blush a little before I turn and head to the boat so she won't see it. I raise my hand and call over my shoulder. "See you at lunch!"

When I reach the boat, Pax takes one look at me and chuckles. Mike stands and looks at us as I glare at my brother.

"What's so funny?" Mike asks before looking at his daughter. "Sarah, run back to Mommy. I'll see you at lunch." She squeezes his leg and runs back toward the house, her blonde curls bouncing off her shoulders.

"My brother is a little starstruck by your wife."

"Pax," I warn, not excited for Mike to know that information.

He claps me on my back and grins. "Don't worry, man, you're not the first and won't be the last. I'm a lucky man." *Yes, he is.* We load up and set off to catch some fish.

The morning is awesome. Although it's hot, we're catching fish left and right, but time spent in their company is always good no matter how fruitful the fishing.

"So what are your plans for work now that you're out of the Air Force?" Mike asks me as he casts again.

"I'm still trying to figure that out. I have interviews in Miami, Jacksonville, Orlando, and Tampa in the next couple of weeks. With my communications degree and my security experience in the Air Force, cyber security seems to be what I'm getting the most interviews for, although I have programming and surveillance experience. It's a matter of who likes me and what cities I like. I want to live in Florida which has limited me a little. I've lived where the Air Force told me to for far too long, and I'm excited to finally choose for myself."

"I get it. Dev and Lucianna are still in Miami and Tommy and Simone are in Tampa if you need somewhere to crash when you're out of town. I know they won't mind."

"I hadn't thought about it, but I'll reach out." Dev works with Mike and Pax, but lives in Miami where his wife is an entertainment lawyer. Everyone who works at Sunset Security with my brother is a veteran, and I haven't met one I don't like yet. Lucianna is Dev's super sexy wife who has more spunk in her pinky finger than most women have in their whole body.

"I may not stay in Tampa. That's easy enough to drive to and from in one day, but I'll see if they want to have a drink or something the day I'm there. I saw where Simone released a new book last week. Looks like she's doing well." Simone is a romance novelist—also Summer's best friend—who is married to Mike Wade's brother Thomas.

"She and Summer were on the phone squealing when she made the USA Today Bestseller list, so I'll say with relative confidence things are going well."

Once we dock and unload the boat, we all jump off the retention wall into the cool water of the Crystal River. "Whooop!" Pax yells when he surfaces. "I always forget how damn cold this water is until I go under the first time."

We laugh at him because he says what we're all thinking and climb out. By the time we're dried off it's time for lunch. I run my fingers through my hair and pull on a clean Sodium Fishing Gear shirt. My phone rings as I'm shoving it into my pocket so I glance at the screen to see it's my buddy, Chance. I click the button to connect the call. "Hey, dude! What's up?" I ask in lieu of a formal hello.

He chuckles. "Aye, Mate. Making sure you're still alive. You never called me last week so I was just checking on ya." His thick Australian accent makes me feel like I'm in a scene in the Crocodile Hunter show.

"Sorry. I got to my brother's house and between the kids and my family it slipped my mind. Everything okay with you and Aubrey?"

"Of course. You find a job yet?"

"No, still looking, but only in Florida. I decided I want to be close to the family, even if that puts me on the other side of the continent from you and Aubrey."

"Damn it, Mate. I thought for sure the last kiss you got from Mutton had you rethinking that." He jokes and I laugh out loud.

"Sorry, buddy, but there has to be more incentive than goat breath for me to be that far from family again,"

"I get it, I get it." His resigned sigh that follows is only half in jest. After Christy, the ex girlfriend, and I broke up, I took a week off work and rode my Harley Davidson Road King to California to clear my head. Would have been a great trip, but some idiot in a sports car ran me off the road in Temecula, California. I had to get it fixed before I rode home and happened to call Chance's shop. He took one look at me and knew I had more than some road rash and a beat-up bike. He set me up in a hotel nearby, and he and Aubrey had me over for dinner one night. A great friendship has built up since then.

Although, I appreciate his and Aubrey's friendship and enjoy every minute I'm with them, I don't want to miss my nieces and nephews growing up. The best way to make sure that doesn't happen is to live nearby. "Listen, I'm headed to lunch can I catch up with you later?"

"Yeah, just give me a ring when you have time."

We disconnect and then we take the two-minute drive to the Lobster Lounge. We're the first in our group to arrive, so we spread out at our table and wait. Mike stops by the bar and brings us over a bucket of beer to get us started. Hudson comes through the doors and slides into the seat next to me. Stacey, his wife, works here and is usually our server.

"Hey, man. Mike bought a bucket of beer, help yourself." I offer Hudson.

"Thanks, Ferris. How was fishing?"

I flash him a grin and answer. "Good. Hot, but I'd rather be cooking like a Thanksgiving turkey and have a line in the water than be anywhere else."

"Ain't that the truth." He agrees and takes a swig of beer.

"Why didn't you come out with us? We had room." I ask.

"I was on toddler duty. Lauren, our babysitter, wasn't available until eleven thirty so I figured I'd just meet y'all for lunch. My boy is a handful in public these days. I never knew something so small could wear you out so much." He shakes his head, and I realize I've never heard him say that many words at one time. Hudson is generally quiet, mostly an observer of people, but I think having a wife and kid has opened him up a bit.

Pax returns from a trip to the bathroom, sits down, and grins at Hudson. "Connor driving you nuts?"

"Yeah, man. That kid has more energy than anyone I've ever known. I thought Sarah Wade was a handful until Connor was born, now I know she's laid back."

We all laugh because Sarah is anything but laid back, so I can't imagine what he's dealing with. Though I'm a bit envious of him. A wife like Stacey, a son, a home, and a great job that fits him to a tee, that's my dream. I'm the kind of guy who enjoys family life. It probably has to do with losing my family so young, my time in foster care and then being brought into a family like the Pearsals.

When I date now it's because I'm trying to see where things will go, if we're compatible, if there's attraction, if it could work in the long run. Most guys my age are looking to get laid. Don't get me wrong. I have a healthy libido, and even being on the nerdy side, I haven't had a problem finding bed partners. You'd be surprised at the number of women who find nerdy a total turn on, but I've grown out of getting laid just for the release in the moment. I'm looking toward the future and won't waste time on anyone who doesn't have that kind of potential.

Stacey approaches the table, and sets another bucket of beer in the middle of the table. "Connor will settle down as he grows up. I hope."

Hudson and Pax look at each other and shake their heads before Hudson looks back at his wife. "Nope, babe, I hate to tell you, but that wild spirit will probably be part of his personality forever."

She must see how serious he is about the subject because she grumbles, "Shit, now I need a beer," and moves back to the bar to grab a tray of drinks for a table behind ours.

"I need to wash up. I'll be right back," I inform the guys as I stand and push my chair in.

I stride through the room toward the bathroom, and as I turn the corner a small but fast-moving person crashes into me. I grasp her shoulders in an attempt to keep her upright. It's Toni, the server I had the last time I was here

"Oh man, I'm so sorry!" she sputters.

I release her when I'm certain she won't tumble over and

take a step back. A quick once over tells me she's not injured from our collision, but she's visibly upset. Her sage-colored eyes are rimmed in red like she's been crying. Her light floral perfume wraps around me, making me pay a different kind of attention to her. It's easy to overlook her when she's moving around the restaurant, but when her body was pressed against mine I realized that although she's slight, she still has a few curves. Her alabaster skin, that probably hasn't seen the sun in quite some time, is soft and smooth. I wonder if she feels that way all over. Today she's wearing black framed glasses that give off that naughty librarian vibe most men have dreams about and for once I'm not immune to that particular fantasy.

"Are you okay?" I ask, wondering if she'll answer. She seemed skittish when she waited on us last time. Her spine straightens, and she lifts her glasses to swipe her finger under her eyes before she responds. "Yeah, I'm good. Just got something in my eye. Sorry I almost ran you over." Her deeper-than-normal-for-a-girl voice sends a sexy vibration down my spine. She gives me a quick smile you can tell is reserved for customers when she's trying to be polite but not in the mood and darts around me back to the kitchen.

I stand frozen for longer than I should, wondering how I missed all those little things at dinner the other night. Finally, I force myself to continue to the bathroom and wash my hands before heading back to the table. Upon my return I smile because Summer, Sarah, Shay, Linc and Morgan have arrived, filling up our table and kicking the noise level up a decibel or two in this place.

When Stacey comes over to take our orders I ask, "What's the deal with that waitress Toni?"

"You might know her from school. She's from Ocala." I knew that. Paxton recognized her before and mentioned it when we had dinner that night, but I didn't think much about it at the time. My mind keeps shifting back to her and I search the room for her because there is something else about her that has me curious. I'm just not sure what it is. I study her as discreetly as possible through the remainder of lunch. Knowing we went to school with her hasn't triggered anything for me, but I can't stop my thoughts and my eyes from veering back to her. There's a weird combination of strength and vulnerability in her eyes you don't see in many people. I'm drawn to strong women.

My birth mother was a formidable woman who worked hard and loved even harder. She was never sitting still. Always busy doing something, and usually it was to help someone else. My adoptive mom, Audrey, and my sister, Courtney, are the same. I will say though, that it's the vulnerability I saw for that split second before she hid it that intrigued my protective instinct. I keep waiting for my brother to catch on and start messing with me. Like all siblings do, the teasing can be relentless at times. Even at our ages.

At the end of the meal, while we are waiting on our checks, my memory bank finally engages when Toni steps out of the kitchen, pauses, runs her fingers through her hair one time and then pulls it up into a ponytail. Recognition flares at that movement and sets off a series of flashbacks that run through my mind in rapid succession.

Toni across the cafeteria running her fingers through her long, dark hair.

Toni walking around the track during P.E., running her fingers through the strands of her hair in order to pull it up in a ponytail.

Toni sitting across the room in science aimlessly

running her fingers through her hair and staring out the window instead of listening to the chemistry lecture.

The thoughts go on and on like that for a full minute, I'm sure. An hour ago, I didn't remember her from school, now I can't figure out how I didn't. Granted she's filled out around her hips and breasts, not that it looks bad, she just doesn't have the body of young girl anymore, and she hasn't kept up with the highlighted sections of her hair like she used to. There's also no sign of her designer duds she wore to school every day, or the full face of makeup she never seemed to leave home without. Just that same signature red lipstick from our high school days artfully applied to her full lips.

I'm thinking the last few years haven't been kind to her, especially if the horse princess is waiting tables at this place. Her family owned a trucking company and a horse ranch so I'm trying to figure out why she's working here.

Pax smacks me on my back, jolting me out of my thoughts and memories. "Come on, dude. We need to get Morgan home for a nap, and Linc wants us to take him to the creek."

I shake my head a little to clear it but take an extra second to study Toni. "Sure. Yeah. Okay."

Pax pauses and turns to see what has my attention. "Toni? The waitress? I wondered why you seemed out in left field during lunch."

"What? Who, me? No way. Come on. Let's go." My brother's eyes squint as he stares at her. He shakes his head and turns to leave.

≈

THAT NIGHT when the kids are in bed, me, Pax, and Shay are watching television and talking. "Have you thought about applying at Sunset Security?"

"Where you work?" I ask, a little surprised by his question.

"Yeah. Mike asked me about it."

"No." I look down at myself. I'm tall and lean with some muscle, but I'm nothing like Mike, Pax, Thomas, Dev, and especially Hudson. "I don't exactly fit the mold or have the tactical training you guys have."

"What mold?" He scoffs.

"Brawny, special ops guy who could snap you in half with a twist of the wrist."

"He's got a point, honey," she agrees but then turns to me. "Though I have to be honest. A black belt in Jiu Jitsu and a lean muscled body is nothing to turn your nose up at. Those are different kinds of strengths. How many bulky MMA fighters have you seen? Not many. It's hard to be fast when you're bulky. Don't shortchange yourself." She smiles at me, and I'm reminded why she's perfect for my brother. Not only is she pretty, but she's also kind, all the way down to her soul.

"That's what I mean. Besides we need members of the team that aren't knocking down doors and wrestling dudes to the ground. We need someone who can handle communications equipment, computer security stuff, and video equipment."

"That would be me tagging along with you like I always have. Aren't we passed that yet?" I ask quietly, the tone of my voice tense beyond joking and on to serious. I always worried when we were young that Pax would get sick of me. We may have had separate friends and interests in school, but I still tagged along quite a bit. And I even prefer to stay with him when I'm in Florida. I think part of that has to do with him proving he always has my back no matter what. It's been that way since the moment we met.

A throw pillow sails through the air straight at my head, but I snag it easily and pull it to my lap. "Don't be dense. There hasn't been a day I considered you tagging along with me a nuisance. We've been friends since day one and brothers since before mom and dad signed the paperwork. Now, I won't pressure you into working somewhere you have no interest in, but I will let you know there is interest from Mike about having you on the team. If it's even a possibility you should put in your application and see what happens. If not, we keep going as we have been."

"I'll think about it," I grumble.

"Works for me. Now tell me why you were staring at the woman who works with Stacey, and don't give me that line of bullshit that you thought she looked familiar. We already established she went to school with us."

That was a slick subject change. Damn him.

"It was nothing. My brain just finally remembered her from when we were in school."

My brother seems to contemplate my response for a moment. "I can't believe you didn't remember her; she was a stunner. She rode horses or something. If I remember correctly, she dated a couple of guys but all of them were douchebags."

"That's her. Pretty girl but in a different league than me back then."

He chuckles. "Only because she didn't have black fingernails and lipstick." I punch him in the arm playfully and scowl as he continues. "Her family did have money. Strange that she's working at the Lobster Lounge now. I never would've taken her for the type to have an actual job, much less one serving other people. I thought her daddy would take care of her forever."

"Yeah, I thought the same. It's strange." What would make her want to waitress at a little restaurant in a small town?

4

TONI

W hen I make it back to my place after my shift, I can hear him before I even enter. "I gotta get out of here! You gotta help me! Make my feet small so I can fit in my shoes! Help me! I have to get out of here," my dad yells at the top of his lungs. This happens every time I end up working later than expected. I should leave the Ativan for Gigi to help him calm down, but I don't truly trust anyone. There are too many horror stories of caregivers stealing a patient's medications. After Lenny screwed my family over so royally, and he was my husband, it's hard to believe an outsider won't do the same. Dementia at this stage of the disease is hard to deal with but without the Ativan it's impossible. So I keep it under lock and key and I'm the only one with a key.

I unlock the door and push inside. My dad is standing buck naked in the hallway, I guess standing is a relative term considering he's leaning heavily on his walker trying to push past Gigi who is blocking his way.

I shut the door and do my best to keep my eyes on my

dad's face. He was a proud man and would be embarrassed if he really understood what was going on.

"Dad, come on, let's get you dressed."

"I don't need to be dressed. I just need my shoes! We have to get out of here! I want to go home. I'm tired of this place and ready to go home! Your mom is waiting on us. She's going to be mad if I bring you home late."

"Oh, Dad. We won't be late. Come on, let's get you dressed, and we can find you a pair of shoes that fit. You can't go anywhere naked. Mom won't like that." I learned not to argue with him when he's like this. I go along with whatever he's saying and find ways to work with the narrative.

"Someone shrunk them all! I can't fit into any."

"Tomorrow, we can go to the store and get you more," I tell him, knowing his shoes still fit, but his brain is so confused he won't understand if I try to explain to him that he's trying to wear my shoes. Lord knows I don't want him going outside in this state. There have been times, usually during daylight hours, when he starts this whole argument of being trapped that I will put him in the car and drive around for a while to clear out the cobwebs and give him different scenery. I won't do it at night because his confusion is greater—the experts call it sundowners syndrome—and I don't want to be fighting with him in our dark driveway.

Once he's turned around, and I have him headed toward his room, I glance over my shoulder at Gigi and mouth, "I'm sorry."

She shakes her head, the sympathy clear in her eyes. "Don't worry. It's okay. You're home, and he will settle now," she whispers.

"Go ahead and go. I'll lock up once I get him to bed."

"I can wait. I don't want to leave the door unlocked in this neighborhood at night."

I don't argue because she's right. We don't live in the worst neighborhood in town, but it's not the best either, and I don't need any more problems than I already have. An intruder would be bad news.

When we get in dad's room, I tug a t-shirt on over his head and help him step into his underwear and a pair of sleep pants. I dig the lock box out of the closet and retrieve his Ativan. I talk him into taking it. His need to flee our home is now lost in his confusion, and I breathe a sigh of relief when he doesn't argue. Finally, I help him into bed. "Dad, tomorrow morning we can go for a ride and see what's blooming. You always love that. Tonight though, I need you to rest."

"Oh honey, you always take care of me. I like the blooms." He closes his eyes and smiles like he can see the various flowers blooming in his mind. I'm not sure what we will find tomorrow. Summer in Florida is brutal and not conducive to a ton of blooming flowers, but I'll try if it makes him smile like that. "Goodnight, Dad. Happy dreams." I place a soft kiss on his forehead, flick on the nightlight, and walk out to say goodbye to Gigi.

"Gigi, you are a lifesaver. I'm so sorry he gave you trouble tonight."

Her soft, cool hand cups my cheek. "You're a sweet girl. It's okay. I knew what I was in for when I took this job. He's not my first dementia client. I worry more about you. There's no one to take care of you. You work hard and then you come home and work harder. A beautiful girl your age should be having fun and enjoying the attention of the young men."

"That sounds lovely, but I've read all the literature, and I know my time with my dad is limited. I'm happy to spend this time with him even if it's only actually him half the time. There will be time for other things when he's gone."

"You're a good daughter. You'll have no regrets."

My smile in response to her compliment is probably a little sad. I don't feel like a good daughter. I'm the idiot who married the man who took advantage of my father's impaired state and ruined his business. I should have been keeping a closer eye on things. My ex-husband is a true son of a bitch. Not only was he embezzling money, but he also made an arrangement with some big-time drug dealers to traffic drugs through our business. My dad was slipping so bad mentally my ex-husband was able to do whatever he wanted, and no one was the wiser. I wasn't paying attention because I didn't work at the company, and I was doing everything I could to avoid my husband. Never in my life did I make a worse mistake than marrying him.

When the DEA raided the warehouse, we were all brought in. My dad and my husband in handcuffs and me for questioning. If it weren't for my lawyer, one I hired myself when it all went down, I would be behind bars too. The only reason my dad isn't, is because when they locked him up it became clear quickly that he was not of sound mind. When the prosecutor went through all the accounting, the interviews, and computers, it was obvious my husband was the brains behind it all. Whatever bit of sanity my dad was hanging on to snapped when he was in jail. He hasn't been the same since, and it's been so painful to watch and to know that he must have been pretty bad early on. I was just too selfish to see any of it and too busy hiding from a life I didn't want once I got it.

~

MY DAD IS awake and back to his easy going self. That's not to say that he's totally with it because he's not. At one point he called me my mother's name, not as a mistake but genuinely thinking I was her. Although I loathe my mother, she left my dad for a trucker named Joe several months before everything went down with the business. I don't mind him calling me Beulah but only because he's in a docile, pleasant mood. Though he didn't remember the conversation from last night about going to look for blooming flowers, I decided it would do us both good to get out of the house for a little while before my evening shift.

We load up in my car and begin to drive out into the country. In the city of Crystal River that's not hard to do. Some people complain that there aren't enough things to do or places to eat in this little town, but I happen to like that you can drive for five or ten minutes to escape the little bit of traffic we have. To me, the fact that you can take a turn down a dirt road and drive for a while without seeing a soul is relaxing. It's peaceful and quaint.

When we set out I couldn't decide if I wanted to keep heading north on highway 19 over the barge canal into Inglis, or if I wanted to get lost down some local dirt roads. But when I stopped at a roadside stand selling boiled peanuts, the man running the stand told me there were a ton of wild blackberry bushes down one of the roads leading to Gator Creek, and I was welcome to pick as many as I wanted. That made up my mind. My mom didn't teach me much, but she did teach me how to make the perfect blackberry cobbler, which will be a nice treat for Gigi and my dad this evening while I'm at work.

About a half mile down the road, I spot two men jogging shirtless in running shorts and sneakers. One is very tan with a set of massive shoulders, muscular legs, and a tiny waist. The other is tall and lean with much lighter skin. Although the second guy is thinner, he isn't less muscled. Both are a beautiful example of the male form glistening with sweat. It's been a while since I noticed anyone and thought about what it might be like to be up close and personal with masculine muscled bodies like either of those guys. Where were guys like this when I was looking? Probably married or from out of town.

I slow down the car so I won't kick a bunch of dust all over them and move to the other side of the road.

"They look awfully hot, Toni," my dad comments as he stares at the men as we pass.

"Yes, they do, Dad," I reply as I glance over lifting a hand in a quick gesture to say hello. Both guys nod their heads and smile, and I'm struck silly for a moment. First of all, the smiles are to die for. Secondly, I realize the two men are Paxton and Ferris. Wow, they shouldn't be let out of the house looking like that. Third, I had no idea Ferris was packing that kind of physique under his clothes. He came across as an average joe sitting next to his brother at the table, and I was too upset when I crashed into him at the restaurant to register what I ran into. I thought he probably looked like any other guy under his clothes. Nothing wrong with him, but certainly not all that. I click up the AC one more notch because the sight of those two got my blood pumping a bit, and I'm suddenly feeling a little warmer than I did a minute ago.

Another mile down the road, I finally see what the man at the boiled peanut stand was talking about. Huge, full blackberry bushes come into sight growing along the fencing as far down as I can see. My heart leaps. "Look at all those blackberry bushes. We're going to have an awesome cobbler tonight."

"Oh my goodness, there are a lot of 'em."

I pull over to the side of the road, leaving enough room for my dad to get out, before I dig around in my back seat and find an old Publix grocery bag. Then I help my dad from the car and set up his walker so he has something to lean on as he waits for me. I begin filling up my bag and talking to my dad as I go. It shouldn't make me so happy to be doing this. I mean I'm standing on the side of a dirt road at ten in the morning with the already oppressive heat and humidity weighing me down. That's crazy. It must be the thought of picking these myself and making something that brings my dad so much joy, that feels so good.

I pause to walk over to my dad. "Okay, try one for me. I need to know they aren't poisonous," I joke, pulling a smile from him. He takes his handkerchief out of his shirt pocket and wipes his face off before reaching into the bag and taking a couple of the beautiful berries. He pops two in his mouth and closes his eyes as if savoring the taste. "I don't know. They could be poisonous. Give me a few more to be sure."

I laugh loudly surprised by my dad's joking mood this morning. We don't get many of these anymore. I hold out the bag, and he grabs more, passing me a couple. I place them on my tongue and bite down, and just like him I close my eyes enjoying everything about this moment. Committing it to memory. I open my eyes again, and we smile at each other, and for a minute all is right in my world. It's as simple as that.

All those years we had money flowing from all sides. We had a beautiful ranch home on twenty acres with a stable full of horses I could ride whenever I wanted. We had nice cars, and nice clothes, and a very good life, but I never appreciated it as much as I appreciate this exact moment.

"I love you, Dad." I tell him with a grin.

"I love you too, honey." His smile is even bigger than mine, and I wish that he could hold on to this memory like I will, but I know that isn't possible.

The pounding of feet on dirt draws my attention away before I have a chance to grow sad about what's to come with my dad. Paxton and Ferris have finally made it to us and instead of jogging right past they stop.

"Hey, you guys okay?" Paxton asks as Ferris observes.

"Oh, yeah. The peanut guy on the side of highway 19 told us that there were a bunch of wild black berries down this road we could pick, so we came to check it out. We're almost done."

"Toni, right?" Paxton asks.

"Yeah, I wasn't sure if you guys would recognize me out of my uniform and on the side of the road."

"I may forget a name but never a face, and my brother" —he points his thumb toward Ferris—"never forgets either one."

They both smile at me, and my stomach does a little flip. "This is my dad, Paul. Dad this is Paxton and his brother Ferris."

Both men shake my dad's hand, I notice they both try to slyly assess the situation with his walker. He certainly doesn't seem old or feeble enough to need one, but like everything else with this disease it has robbed him of basic functions, and one of those is stability while he walks. Although he doesn't always need it, I've gotten him used to using it all the time just in case.

"Did y'all bring water? It's awfully hot to be out here without it," Paxton notes.

"No, I just thought we were going to ride around for a little while. I had no intention of hanging out in the heat today." I chuckle softly and look away. They must think I'm an idiot. Who just drives around for the hell of it or stops on the side of the road to pick blackberries that aren't theirs? A crazy person, that's who.

"Well, come on by the house. I have some bottled water I can give you. Then I won't worry you'll pass out while you're out here," Paxton continues.

"No, it's okay. I don't want to impose. I shouldn't even be picking these. I don't know who the land belongs to, but I couldn't resist. It's been a while since I've had wild black-berries."

"Don't worry about it. My wife will kick my butt if I don't make sure you come by. Besides, we have a ton of these bushes running along the front of our property. I don't know who owns these, although out here I doubt they would care if you were eating them, but I do know who owns mine, and we would love to put them to good use. We can't eat enough of them, and they rot if you don't eat them fast enough."

"I could use some water," my dad says from behind me, and I glance back to see him wiping the sweat away with his handkerchief again. Damn it. My poor dad.

"Okay, where do we go? Do you want a ride the rest of the way?"

Both men laugh and shake their heads. "Nah, we need to finish this run. Go up to the next dirt road and turn right. We are the first driveway on the left. We should be home in about ten minutes."

"Thank you." I tell them before they turn and continue their run. Ferris never said a word during that whole exchange. He wore a smile I can only describe as cocky as he watched my father and I like he was cataloging some-thing. If he sat with a sketch artist after this meeting I bet he could have us drawn up to a tee. I'm wondering if he's suspicious of us or something. I guess it is weird that we're on a random dirt road picking blackberries.

I take my time picking some more and then getting my dad back into the car to give the guys some time to make it back to the house. I'm hoping he gives his wife a little warning that we are on our way so we don't surprise them.

When we drive down the long dirt driveway, a beautiful ranch style home comes into view with the most perfect front porch complete with a swing and rocking chairs. It's something you would see in an old painting of the south but with a more modern brick and stucco home. I'm instantly jealous of the family inside and the perfect life they must be living.

Before we even get out of the car, Lincoln, the boy from dinner, swings the front door open and turns to shout something inside. A moment later, Shay comes to the door with a grin on her face and holds the door open.

I guide my dad to the railing and set the walker aside. Then I stand on his other side and encourage him to take one step at a time up the couple of steps to the porch. Shay holds the door open. "Come on in, it's too hot to sit out here in the rockers this time of day."

"I hate to impose," I tell her.

"Don't worry about it. I love to have company, and I just finished laundry, so I had nothing to do anyway. Come in and have a seat."

I lead my dad through the open floor plan living area to a couch and make sure he's seated comfortably before I sit next to him. Shay glances over at Lincoln who is watching my dad with curiosity. "Hey, bud. Can you go get them some bottled waters? I'm sure they're thirsty."

"Yes, ma'am," he politely replies and we watch as he hurries across the room, around the kitchen island, and reaches inside the refrigerator. We haven't even started talking when he returns, thrusting our waters toward us with excitement.

Shay's smile is bright as she opens the conversation. "Pax said y'all were picking blackberries. We used to do that for hours when we were kids and then run down to the creek to cool off after we dropped off our full buckets at my house. We both sort of grew up out here, so we know the draw of those sweet berries."

"We were just out driving around. Sometimes I need to get dad out of the house. We stopped to buy some boiled peanuts from the vendor on the side of highway 19, and he told us about the blackberries. I make a killer blackberry cobbler and couldn't resist. I should have been more careful. It's not good having him out in the heat like this."

Shay glances at my dad with an expression I can only describe as understanding. "Being secluded at home is no fun. It's sweet that you brought him out here. You should do it more often, especially when I'm home. I work during the week at Sunset Security, but we're here on the weekends, at least until baseball season starts up again. Then it's hit or miss. I'll give you my number so we can text and set it up."

Warmth spreads in my chest, and I can't help but smile at her. It's been so long since I've had more than one friend that I can't help but be hopeful. Especially since she realizes just by looking at us that my situation is not easy and includes my dad. I don't think she figured out the extent of his illness, but she knows something is wrong. Dad hasn't spoken since we arrived but doesn't seem to be unhappy. In fact, by the serene expression on his face I would venture to say he's relaxed.

I pat his leg softly. "Dad, drink your water. I don't want you to get dehydrated." He looks over at me a little surprised, and I nod down to the water in his hand resting on his thigh. I'm thankful he was given bottled water with a cap, so it won't accidentally spill on the furniture when he inevitably forgets it again.

"Oh, how nice, you got me water." He grins at me.

"No, Dad. Lincoln got it for you. Shay's son." I gesture toward the young man sitting across from him looking a little confused.

"Oh, thank you, young man. I must have been daydreaming."

"It's okay, Dad, just drink the water, please." The sound of footfalls coming from the hallway draws my attention, and I discover Ferris coming out from the hallway. It's a little harder to concentrate on his face when I know what's under the T-shirt and longer shorts now. I wonder why he hides his beautiful physique. Pax opens a door to the right and comes out right after. His shirt is pulled tight across his broad shoulders and bulging muscles. He is either showing off his physique or can't find shirts that fit any looser. By the way his wife is staring at him though, I have a feeling it may just be to keep her attention.

My dad focuses on Ferris for some reason and blurts, "I've seen you before."

Ferris smiles at him, and my heart flutters a little. His smile is a little crooked because one side lifts higher than the other, but it's the little crinkle beside his eyes of genuine amusement that gets to me.

"About fifteen minutes ago, I saw you picking blackberries while I was jogging."

"Oh yeah." My dad seems genuinely happy about that. "Yes, yes, now I remember. You reminded me of my father when he was young. Lean and muscular, the perfect example of a middle weight boxer."

Ferris laughs as he pauses to talk. "I'll take that as a compliment. But I'm not a boxer."

"No, he's not, but he kills it at Ju Jitsu," Pax cuts in.

"What's Ju Jitsu?" Lincoln asks.

"It's a form of martial arts, but it's more on the ground and uses leverage, pressure, and angles to get the job done," Ferris answers.

Lincoln looks at him blankly for a moment before Ferris expands his explanation. "It's a type of karate but you're wrestling on the ground more than you're up kicking or karate chopping someone." There's humor in his voice this time.

"Sounds kind of weird." Lincoln's honesty makes us all laugh.

"Yeah, it is, but I wasn't like your dad growing up, all big and burly like a bear. I was small and scrawny and needed to defend myself, so your grandpa got me started in Ju Jitsu. It's helped me out of a lot of bad situations, and it's good for teaching your body and mind strength and discipline."

"Is that how you got all muscly?" Lincoln asks, and we crack up again.

"Yeah, Linc, that's how I got my muscles." Ferris runs his hand affectionately over the top of the boy's head as he sits down next to him.

"Your dad was a boxer?" Lincoln aims the question at my dad, and I watch his face brighten.

"Yes, boy. My dad was a great boxer. Tough as nails, my old man. He could drop 'em left and right."

"He sounds pretty cool." Lincoln grins at him.

"I wish you could meet him. He's been gone a while though. Before I even married my wife."

"You're married?" Linc inquires.

My dad says yes at the same time I say no. He was so

lucid there for a moment talking about his dad I forgot he slips in and out at times and seems to remember things from thirty years ago easier than he does things from this week.

My dad's surprised eyes connect with mine, and I inwardly curse this disease. "Dad, you and mom have been divorced almost two years now."

"We have?" The confusion in his voice makes my heart sink.

"Yeah." I squeeze his hand gently.

I glance at the group quickly. "Sorry, Dad is forgetful sometimes. They're divorced. He lives with me. We do pretty well together." I hold his hand a little tighter, hoping he knows I mean it. As tiring as it is and as often as he gives me fits, I still wouldn't have it any other way.

"You've always taken care of me, little girl. We can talk about Beulah later." My dad releases my hand and pats my leg. Any time he asks about her we have to relive the whole thing over again, and I'd rather not. It's painful to watch his heart break over and over. As for me, I gave up on my mom a long time ago. She was too busy with her own life to have anything to do with mine.

"Not always, but I try."

"You're a good girl." His whole face softens when he looks at me. I'll miss these moments with him when he's gone mentally. I'm thankful I have these little pieces of lucidity for now though. They help me get through the times when he has no clue who I am or what is happening."

Lincoln interrupts our conversation. "Uncle Ferris, I thought you were a computer nerd. I didn't know you were some kind of secret ninja."

Shay gasps, her eyes going wide. Ferris grabs Linc in a head lock and gives him a noogie on his head while the boy squeals with laughter. "I'm way cooler than a computer nerd," he teasingly scolds his nephew. Laughter breaks out around the room for a moment until Ferris releases him. It was a good way to end that awkward tender moment I had with my dad before I started to cry in a room full of people I barely know.

"Computer nerd?" I ask, curious about this guy. I'm getting the sense he's a man of many layers, and you have to work to see each one. I realize he probably lived in Pax's shadow because that man commands the presence of the room just by his sheer size and level of confidence. Ferris is probably underestimated quite often which makes him more intriguing.

"Yeah, I've always been into computers and gaming. They like to tease me a lot. None of my siblings are into that stuff."

Pax's deep voice pipes up. "That computer stuff is about to come in handy in your career, and also one of the reasons Sunset Security wants you to work for us." You can hear the pride in his voice. He's proud of his brother and doesn't like him being thought of as less because he's a computer guy.

"They want me because of you."

"Bullshit. You have the hands-on security and military experience Mike likes our guys to have an unparalleled understanding of computer programming, wiring, and technology. He wants you because you're a techie badass."

Ferris is the first one to chuckle before we all join in. "That is true. Should I put that under qualifications on my job applications?"

"Honey, I'm not sure I've ever heard anyone put it quite that way. 'Techie badass'." Then Shay breaks down in peals of laughter. Pax's hands are clenched tight, and his anger is almost palpable.

"Lighten up, big brother. You don't have to protect me from being who I am. I'm okay being a techie bad ass." He chuckles as he says those last words. "I'm comfortable in my own skin. You helped me get there over the years. But seriously, that was funny."

Pax's fists relax, and he rolls his eyes. "You know—" he starts to respond before Ferris cuts him off.

"Yeah, I know. I'm cool. It's all good."

For this being a quick stop for a drink of water there have been some heavy things discussed in this room, probably more than I can take for the day. "Okay, Dad. Let's get your water and go home. Gigi is coming soon, and I need to get ready for work."

I turn my attention to everyone else in the room. "Thank you so much for the water and the company. Your home is lovely as is your family."

We all stand, and I put dad's walker in front of him. Shay rushes over to the counter and scribbles something on a note pad, tears the paper off, and brings it over to me.

"Please give me a call sometime. I would love to have you both back out here. And if you find yourself picking blackberries again, you know you can stop in for a cold water."

A cry from the back of the house followed by a loud call for mommy has Shay excusing herself to go to Morgan who must have been napping.

5

FERRIS

For several hours after Toni and Paul left, all I could think about was her. I'm guessing her father has Alzheimer's or something by the memory issues. I mean, how do you not remember you're divorced? Thank God my family is cool enough to let it slide. Even Linc, who is still a kid, understood not to ask too many questions about it. Toni is clearly not the woman I remember her to be from high, not that most of us are like we were back then anyway, but it's still a relief. It's not that she was a bitch, in fact she could have been sweet and kind once you got to know her. But in high school, a girl like her, who everyone knew, who had money and not a problem in the world it seemed, she would never have given a pimple-faced geek like me a second look, even as a friend. I'm not bitter, I'm just thinking in factual high school terms. Now, Pax, she would have given him the time of day. Hell, all the girls did. Today she seemed grateful for the water and the company. I wonder if she has any other family that help her with her dad. She said he lives with her, but if he does have some kind of failing condition, I don't know how she would do it without help. Especially considering she works full-time.

After a swim in the creek with Linc and Morgan and a quick review of the companies I will be interviewing with this week, I'm feeling antsy. I head to the living room where Pax is playing with Morgan on the floor, and Shay is folding laundry. "I think I'm going to head into to town for a beer and a change of scenery. Either of you want to go with me?"

"Nah man, sorry. I want to spend some time with the family since I'll be traveling for work this week."

"I'm out too. Want to hang with the big guy while he's home. Sorry, Ferris, though, the rest of the week you're stuck entertaining me."

I grin at her. She's plenty busy without me entertaining her, but because our backgrounds are very similar we understand each other like no one else does. Although her family didn't die in a house fire, they did die in an equally tragic way. Her mom, dad, and younger sister were shot to death in their home one night while Shay was staying with her grandmother. Something like that changes you in a way no one that hasn't lived it can understand. "No problem, just thought I'd ask. I'll make sure I get my talking points ready for the week," I joke and then add, "See you later."

I grab my keys off the hook by the front door and head out the door. When I hit town I note a couple of my favorite bars, but I drive past and keep going. I'm feeling restless and have no idea why. I tend to be pretty chill most of the time, so the restlessness is a bit unnerving. When I get to the border between Homosassa and Crystal River, I turn around and head back north on highway 19. I turn down a side road and before I know it, I'm in the parking lot for the Lobster Lounge, and the only thing I can think about is if Toni is wearing the red lipstick tonight. It's a stupid thing to think about, but she has such a perfectly shaped mouth. Full, but not too much so, and her upper lip is arched like a bow, so when she wears the red lipstick it's all I can focus on when I talk to her. In all my memories of her she's wearing that shade of lipstick so it's a poor excuse to turn up at the Lobster Lounge to see if she's wearing it.

Before I can change my mind and leave, I stride to the entrance and pass through the doors. Once inside, I grab a seat at the bar and get a pint of Marker 48's Red Right Return. The bartender is the same guy that's been here the last few times I've been here with my brother. He must recognize me too because he asks, "Where's Paxton tonight? I thought you two were joined at the hip since you came home from the Air Force."

"We have been, but I needed a beer and a change of scenery. I also thought it might give him some time with his family without me in the middle of it."

"I doubt your brother cares. He seems pretty laid back."

"He is, and he probably doesn't care, but I still want to be respectful." Changing the subject I inquire, "Have you been busy tonight? It seems kind of slow for a Sunday evening."

"Our rush was earlier. It died off a little after eight which is good. Scallop season is kicking my ass. We've had a lot of late nights the last few weeks with all the people in the area on vacation."

As he's finishing his sentence, the woman I haven't been able to stop thinking about all day approaches the bar with her head down looking at the orders on her pad.

"Hey Nick, I need a margarita on the rocks, no salt, a tequila sunrise top shelf, and a Red Right Return. She lifts her head to confirm he got that and finally notices me. Her fire engine red lips tilt up at the corners. "Fancy seeing you here tonight. I would say you're stalking me, but I did come to your house today, so that's not accurate."

"Yeah, it does seem a little fishy with me turning up here, doesn't it?" I smile and think about what a dork I sound like. Flirting has never been my strong suit, but I find myself wishing it were as I stand here with her full attention.

She pushes her glasses back up her nose and winces a little.

"You okay?"

"Yeah, I got a headache this afternoon after I got back home and couldn't get my contacts in, so I threw these goofy things on hoping it would help. It hasn't."

"Did you take anything for your headache?"

"Yeah, but that didn't work either. I'm probably just dehydrated. I'll drink a Gatorade when I get home and hopefully get some sleep."

She turns to go but pauses. "Good to see you again, Ferris. I have to go get the rest of this drink order filled."

Before I can respond she's gone. The next two hours I watch as she hustles around the restaurant. I probably should have headed back to Pax's by now, but I keep sitting here, sipping my beer, hoping to hear her voice again, maybe even make her smile.

Realizing she's probably never going to get a break or think to come back over to me, I head to the men's room before I pay my tab and clear out. On my way back to the bar, raised voices snag my attention. I turn the corner to find Toni backed against the wall while a middle-aged couple are yelling and pointing their fingers in her face. My blood boils in an instant. I can't stand bullies. There's no reason two grown people should have someone backed into a corner like she is, causing her to look like a frightened rabbit. Without thinking I rush toward the group.

"Hey! Back off," I yell, and when they turn to see who dared break up their attack, I roughly maneuver into the little space between them and a tear-streaked Toni. "I don't know what your problem is, but if you don't back off and get out of her face, I'll throw you out those doors so fast you won't know what hit you."

Toni's hands grip my shirt, and I feel her bury her head against my back. I reach back with one hand to soothe her. The man stands up straight and puffs his chest out like that's supposed to scare me. "I'm not going anywhere. Thanks to that bitch and her daddy we had the DEA and FBI crawling all over our house. I lost my job and my house because of their greedy drug dealing bullshit. I've been looking for her, and now that I found her I'm going to make sure she suffers like we did." I do a quick scan of his body language to try to gauge his true anger level. This guy has wild eyes, his hands are clenched and his face is as red as a tomato. This could escalate quickly if I don't squash this.

"That's not true." I hear her say against my back, not loud enough to be aggressive, but loud enough I hear it.

"I don't give a damn what you think she and her father did. If you have an issue call the police. You don't come to her place of work and accost her."

"The police have already been called, and they haven't done anything," angry guy protests.

"Well, there's your answer, and now it's time for you to get out. I'm going to let management know you're harassing their employee, and I'm willing to bet you won't be welcome back here anytime soon." I stand strong as I face him down. I could drop this guy in a half a second, but I'm trying not to make this more embarrassing for Toni than it already is.

"Screw you! If this place employs thieves like her I don't want to eat here anyway."

I step as close to him as I can without touching him, uncomfortably close, and look down at him. I'm not a bulky man like my brother, but I'm tall and am doing my best to show how intimidating I can be. My size doesn't convey the damage I can do if pressed. "Time to shut up and leave."

"You trying to intimidate me?" His machismo won't let him walk away without a fight of some sort.

"Nope, just making sure you can hear me and get my point. I guarantee you don't want me to haul your ass out of here. I can do it, and it won't be pleasant." My hands twitch at my sides. Now that I can see that he's an all-talk-no-action kind of guy, I'm hoping he makes a move. I know he's under-estimating me. Thinking because I'm skinny I can't hand him his ass. It will be my absolute pleasure to show him how wrong he is.

The bartender comes around the corner and stops dead when he sees the situation. "What's going on?" he barks.

"Your employee is a stealing piece of trash. They took my livelihood because they were so greedy! We won't eat here if she keeps working here," the man spits angrily.

My eyes shift to the bartender, waiting to see what he'll do with this, but I don't move anything else. He slides up next to me. "Toni is the hardest working server we have. If you're the sort of bully who shows up to her place of business to try to embarrass her, freak her out, and get her fired then we don't want your business."

Toni keeps hold of the back of my T-shirt and presses her head deeper into my back, the sigh she releases warms my back through my shirt. She was scared she was going to get fired. That boils my blood even more. What an asshole.

I gain more respect for the bartender after seeing how he handled this situation.

"Your manager won't feel the same when we tell him the

story." Two things strike me about his words. First, he automatically assumes the manager is a man, and two, he's not letting this go. Not only is he a jerk, he's also a misogynistic dickhead.

"Actually, we vet our employees carefully. We know the story with her family, none of which has anything to do with her specifically. And I'm the manager. The owner is in the backroom if you'd like me to get him to throw your ass out. I wasn't kidding when I said we don't want your kind here."

I stand even straighter and glare at the jerk and his wife who both look ready to spit nails.

The woman finally grabs the man's hand and tugs on it. "Come on, we don't want to eat somewhere they knowingly employ criminals anyway." They turn and storm out the door, grumbling the whole way.

I make a mental note to stay here until closing to escort her to her car. I won't put it past them to stick around and make more trouble in the parking lot after her shift.

My instinct is to soothe Toni, to take away the fear. I have the overwhelming urge to hold her close and tell her it's going to be okay. By her reaction I'm sure she has the feeling that everything she has is about to disintegrate in her hands, which is something that I remember well. Without thinking how weird it will be or how inappropriate, I turn toward her, dislodging her grip on my T-shirt, and wrap my arms around her.

She stiffens instantly, and I bend my head to whisper, "Relax, they won't hurt you. I'll make sure of it. I'm not leaving until you're safely in your car and on your way home."

The tightness in her body eases, and she sort of melts into my hold. This time it's me who sighs in relief. "Thank you," she whispers, barely loud enough for me to hear. Once again, acting on instinct, I kiss the top of her hair, hoping more than anything to soothe her. She doesn't react.

The bartender pipes up next to me. "Take a few minutes to compose yourself. I'll check on your tables. Don't worry about those assholes. You're too good of a worker to let shit like that affect your job."

She pulls back from my hold, and a chill sweeps over me. One I don't think I've ever felt before. I've had my share of relationships with woman, but none left me feeling like this. I can't even explain it.

Toni's eyes move to the bartender. "Thanks, Nick. It means a lot." Her smile is soft and sincere. He nods once and takes off toward the dining room. She pushes the glasses back up her nose. "I didn't know my bosses knew about my history. I didn't do anything wrong except marry the wrong man and not keep a close enough eye on my father's business. I know I was naïve, but I would never knowingly hurt anyone."

"I believe you. Besides no one deserves to be ambushed like that."

"I need to get back to work. Thank you." Her eyes lower from mine like she's too embarrassed for eye contact. The shame she conveys cements my determination to stick around and see her safely to her car.

I resume my position at the bar, and when it's time to close out my tab so Nick can shut down the bar for the night, he refuses to let me pay. "Man, you were ready to go to battle for one of our ladies. There is no way I'm letting you pay for your drinks tonight. We're a family in this place. No one messes with our people and since you had her back, your money is no good tonight." The soapy water he's washing the glasses in runs down his arm as he continues to chat. "You know, she really is a good person. I can't say what happened wasn't fucked up. It was, but she had nothing to do with it, and from what I can gather her father didn't either. If that piece of shit ex-husband of hers ever shows up here I'll throat punch him after what he's put her through. I hope they convict him and put him away for so long he forgets his name."

I don't say much. I'll do my own research, but the woman I met the other day, the one who was invited into my brother's house today, wouldn't do anything to hurt anyone like they're accusing. I'm decent at reading people, and unless she's a master manipulator I doubt she could do what those people accused her of. Just sounds like she's a terrible judge of character though. Nothing inherently wrong with that except it probably leaves her open to a lot of heartache.

Once Toni is done rolling her silverware and finishing her side work, she grabs her things, and I follow her toward the door. "Let me go out first, just in case. Those people were a little nuts."

I open the door and hold it while facing forward to scan the parking lot. There are only three cars left in the lot. Mine, hers, and either Nick's or the cook because we're the only ones left in the building. At first glance, everything seems okay in the dimly lit parking lot, but as we get closer to her car, I notice that her car is sitting a little funny. I reach behind me and grab her hand. "Something isn't right."

"What do you mean?" Her quiet voice is shaky.

I squeeze her hand, hoping to give a little reassurance, but I stay silent because I don't have an actual answer. A few more steps and it becomes clear. Flat tires. Three of the four are flat.

Son of a bitch!

How did they know which car was hers? "Son of a bitch!" I growl.

"What is it?"

"Flat tires." I do my best to keep my tone even and not convey the absolute insane fury I'm feeling.

"Damn it. I don't have the money to replace a flat tire," her voice trembles.

God, I really hate this. "I'm sorry, Toni. It's three flat tires."

"Three?" she shrieks and steps around me, dropping my hand like a hot potato.

"Yeah. I'll take you—" I begin, but she cuts me off.

"Oh no, no, no, no." It's obvious the hysteria is setting in. She's reached her breaking point. "I just can't win. No matter how hard I try to get ahead, someone always pushes me a step back. This time three steps back. What the hell did I do to earn such bad luck? I mean..." She pauses and begins pacing in front of me like a caged lion. "I mean, I try so hard to do right by my family and myself and the people around me, and still, I'm standing in the parking lot looking at three flat tires from a disgruntled couple who assume things about me that aren't true. I can't take it anymore. I'm so tired." Just when I think she might let out a blood curdling scream, I watch her sag to her knees and the tears flow down her beautiful face.

6

TONI

Scraping my knees and completely losing it in front of someone I barely know is not how I planned to finish the night. A glass of wine in hand with my feet kicked up, listening to my father's snores coming from his bedroom were more of what I was hoping for. Instead, I'm on my knees hysterically crying in my work parking lot. Ferris has to be cursing himself for sticking around to walk me out. Men tend to hate emotional women and drama. Tonight has been nothing but drama, and he's been in it for hours now.

With the gentlest hands and voice I've ever felt or heard from anyone, Ferris lifts me to my feet and scoops me up into his arms like a little kid being carried to bed. "It's okay, Toni. I'll take care of it. No worries. Let me get you home, and I'll come back and handle it." His lips press against my head again, like they did earlier in the evening, and though I feel the comfort the gesture is meant to convey I cry harder. It's been so long since anyone has treated me with tenderness and care. Far too long. His voice vibrates against my cheek as he's talking to someone I can't see.

"Someone slashed her tires. I'm taking her home. I'll come back in the morning and take care of it when the tire place opens."

The other voice, clearly Nick says, "Give me a minute and I can take care of it."

"No, man. It's no big deal. I've got it," Ferris replies.

I fight my emotions and settle the tears to a trickle accompanied by some sniffles. I won't let him handle all this for me. I'll figure something out, but I don't have the energy to argue tonight. As soon as I get home, I'll be able to find some clarity. It's hard to find it when my mind is whirling like it is. I'm resourceful and can deal with it before morning. I lift my head and look around about the time he halts abruptly and curses. Behind us I hear Nick yell, "Those sons a bitches!"

Ferris swears and turns around with me still in his arms. "You too?"

"Yes, those bastards slashed my tires. Yours too?"

"Yup. Give me a minute. I'll call my brother."

"Honey, I'm going to set you on your feet. Do you think you can stand?" I can feel his muscles tighten with building tension, but he's still gentle as he lowers me to my feet. Smoothing his hands down my shoulders as he looks me over. "Give me a minute, I need to call Pax." I nod, but remain quiet, too overwhelmed and exhausted to say anything in return. I've been through worse, and I know I may struggle, but this won't be what kills me.

"Hey, man, sorry to wake you. I need your advice and probably a ride. I'm at the Lobster Lounge. I'll explain everything later, but do you know a local garage with tow service that has a tire shop?" I can only hear Ferris' side of the conversation, but the voice on the other end gets louder.

"I'll see if I can catch a taxi home once they tow the cars.

No, bro, stay with your family. I have this, I'm just not familiar enough with Crystal River to know who to call for this. Yeah, yeah. Okay. Three cars. One of them is my rental. I'll call the rental company for mine. They may want it to go to a specific company."

"Okay, thanks man. I'll wait for you to call back."

Once he disconnects, Nick approaches us. "My wife is on her way to pick me up. I'll take care of this tomorrow. I'm too tired to worry about it tonight."

"If you leave me your keys, I'll handle it. My brother is calling someone to tow it tonight. They can put tires on in the morning and have it ready first thing."

"I can't have you handle this. I'll get it in the morning."

"I'm so sorry, guys. This is my fault."

They both turn to me with almost mirroring images of irritation. "It's not your fault," they reply simultaneously.

Nick glances between the two of us and says, "I'm calling the Sheriff's department in the morning and have them pull the tapes from the bar next door. It should have caught them getting at least one of our cars. Our cameras have been down since the lightning strike fried them last month. Do you know those people's names?"

"No, but I'm sure with video evidence and a list of names of former workers from my dad's company the police could narrow it down easily. But I hate this. Sometimes I hate my life."

Ferris slips an arm around my shoulders and pulls me into his side. Without thinking about it, my arms wrap around his middle and hold tight. I want to use his strength to get through tonight. It could've been worse but not by much. It's about that time a truck pulls into the parking lot and comes to a stop in the parking spot next to Ferris's car.

Mike Wade, a frequent customer, climbs out of the driver side.

"Hey man. You guys okay?" Concern etched in his voice.

"We're good. Just pissed," Ferris responds. "What're you doing here?"

"Your brother called me. I could get here quicker than he can. I called Old Homer to come help. He's getting dressed, and then he'll be here."

"Old Homer. Damn, why didn't I think of that?" Nick murmurs.

"Old Homer?" I ask, wondering who that is.

It's Nick who answers. "I'm sure you've seen him. You just didn't know that was his name. It's the older African American guy who sits at the bar every Sunday with the Tampa Bay Buccaneers hat, shirt, shorts, and orange knee-high socks, cheering when Tampa scores and cursing loudly when they don't. He has a tire shop. Nicest guy in town. Although it's late. He had to be in bed."

"He was, but I wasn't going to let you guys leave your cars here all night. There is no telling what kind of vandalism might happen if those people stuck close by. Don't need to add insult to injury when help is easy to find."

Nick's wife pulls into the parking lot, her hair in a messy knot on top of her head, and her glasses on in place of the contacts she usually wears. "That's my wife." He indicates with a tip of his chin in her direction.

"I'm just going to have Old Homer load the cars up on his flatbed and take them back to his shop. He can switch out the tires first thing in the morning and have them ready for y'all to pick up."

"Thanks, man, I appreciate it. I'm too damn tired to think of a different solution tonight," Nick tells him.

"The Sheriff's office will contact you tomorrow for your

statement. They should be here any minute to file a report. I called them as soon as Pax called me," Mike explains as he glances at his phone.

"Thanks again," Nick says as he turns and moves toward the car.

New headlights bounce as they cross the bump from the road into the parking lot and the shape of the police car becomes obvious. How in the hell did they get here so quickly?

Right behind the police cruiser a truck pulls into the lot, and I swear I hear Ferris breathe a sigh of relief. A couple of seconds later both vehicles are parked, and Paxton's large frame is climbing down from the truck. His door slams, and he approaches our little group at the same time as the cop.

"You guys okay?" Pax asks before the cop can say a word.

"Yeah, we're okay. I know she's probably tired though," Ferris answers his brother.

I shrug, fatigue pulling on my shoulders, but more than anything, I'm embarrassed that my past has followed me to Crystal River. It's different if it's just a story you hear in passing, but when reality is right in your face it's something you can't forget about.

Paxton prowls forward, and by the tick of his clenched jaw and clench of his fists it's obvious he's pissed. I shrink back so I'm partially behind Ferris. Paxton hasn't given me any reason to think he'll freak out on me, but exaggerated rise and fall of his chest and the lowered eyebrows indicate he's ready for a fight. Since this is my fault, I'm certain I'll be on the wrong side of his ire, especially since his brother is involved.

"Hey, it's okay." Ferris glances at me. He wraps his arm around me and pulls me in close like he plans to protect me as Paxton approaches ahead of the Sheriff's deputy.

"You guys okay?" Pax asks as eyes move between us, probably more than a little curious as to why his brother's arm is around a woman he barely knows.

"Yeah, some assholes with a bone to pick, or so we think, slashed her, the bartender's and my tires.

"What the hell?" he barks, his fists clenched at his sides like he's ready to fight.

"It's a long story. You can listen while we talk to the deputy so we don't have to repeat it. Then we can get these vehicles towed to Old Homer's shop and drive her home."

"Fine," he concedes, even though it's obvious he's ready to hear the story now and then go crack some heads.

A moment later the deputy approaches and introduces himself as Sergeant Lane Dawson. We explain what happened earlier with the couple and what we came out to find. He takes our official statements, a bunch of pictures, and then allows Old Homer to load the cars one at a time. Sergeant Dawson explains he'll be in touch in the next couple of days. He plans to pull the security footage from the cameras next door and is hoping they will show something. While we're waiting, I text Gigi to tell her what's going on and let her know I will be home as soon as I can.

Paxton pulls Mike aside for a private conversation. They're talking quietly, but I can still hear the concern in their voices. Great. They're probably trying to find a way to peel Ferris off me and drag him away before I can cause him any more trouble. I mean, who wouldn't be freaked out that their brother and friend is caught in a situation with people who make scenes in restaurants and slash tires? I would tell my brother to run too if I had one. "It's gonna be okay. Just relax," Ferris whispers close to my ear. "You have nothing to worry about."

"It's just embarrassing. I'm pretty sure your brother

wants to throw you in his truck and drive you as far away from me as he can."

"My brother is worried about you. He's not angry at you." I roll my eyes but keep my mouth shut because I don't think Ferris could be reading the situation any more different if he tried.

The deputy says his goodbyes as Old Homer pulls back into the parking lot to pick up the last of the three cars. Mike comes over and pulls out his wallet and hands me a card. "If you have any more problems, please give me a call. I'll be glad to help, and I'll let the other guys know what's going on so that if I'm out of town they can help you."

I'm shocked. I thought for sure he would haul ass out of here to get away from this mess and not look back. "You don't have to do that. I'll be okay," I tell him, praying it's true.

"Paxton tells me you're taking care of your father with ailing health and working. Is that correct?"

I nod, a little surprised that's the information they shared in their little huddle.

"I want to make sure you know you have backup if those people come back or anyone like them. Any sign of them at all, and you call me. Don't pause and think about it. Just call. I only live around the corner and don't mind doing it. You have a lot on your plate and don't need added worry."

"Thanks, Mike. I appreciate it. I can't thank you enough for coming out in the middle of the night to help us. I haven't been here long enough to know who to call to handle a situation like this."

The corner of his mouth twitches. "Well, now you do. Call anytime." He gives Ferris and Paxton a chin lift and strides back to his truck.

Old Homer comes over and gives me and Ferris his business cards, complete with grease-stained fingerprints. He said he thinks he has the tires we need on hand and should have the cars ready by ten in the morning. We thank him before Ferris leads me to Paxton's truck. He helps me inside the passenger seat and closes the door. Then he gets in behind me, and I can hear the seat belt click into place.

Paxton fires up the truck and turns toward me. "Which way is home?"

"Go right out of the parking lot." I give him directions on the short drive to my place, thankful I don't have to sit in the uncomfortable silence for long since it's so close. I'm ready to breathe a sigh of relief when we turn down my street, until I see a familiar silhouette under the streetlight leaned up against a souped-up Mercedes Benz. "Damn it," I whisper to myself.

With the music off and the cab of the truck quiet both men heard my swear. "What's wrong?"

"That's where I live."

I point straight ahead, and Ferris asks, "Who is that waiting by the car?"

Paxton pulls past the car and into the driveway. "That's my ex-husband. I have no idea why he's here. I didn't even know he was out of jail."

As soon as the truck comes to a stop, both men unhook their seat belts. "Is this a welcome guest?" Paxton asks. He obviously can't see that my face has lost all of its color in the dark cab.

"No, not welcome. Not even close. I haven't seen him in almost a year, and I was hoping to make it much longer than that."

"Stay in the truck. I've got this," Paxton informs us.

"Think again, bro," Ferris replies, swings his door open, and climbs out. Paxton curses under his breath and follows his brother. I can hear raised voices as they approach Lenny.

I unbuckle and twist in my seat to get a better look. His hair is cut short on the sides, long and styled on the top. His smile is a little too slick and his words probably too charming for a late-night visit from an ex-husband. I can tell he's using his manipulative bullshit to try and talk these guys down, but neither of them has backed down. In fact, even though their limbs appear to be loose, there is nothing about their stances that indicates they won't take him to the ground if they need too. When it comes to Lenny my mind automatically starts churning with fear and the possibilities of what he can do to them. What if he has a gun? I always knew him to carry one. And if he came looking for me and my dad I'm certain he'll keep his firearm close.

Without thinking I swing the door open and hustle out of the truck toward the group of them. I can't let anything happen to them, especially over me.

"What the hell do you want Lenny?"

"I need to talk to you." He doesn't move a single muscle except to turn his head toward me. I've seen that look too many times to count, and it means he's barely holding his temper in check. My ex is ready to go apeshit on Pax and Ferris.

"I don't want to talk to you. You can go. I'll call the police if you don't leave."

"I'm not going anywhere. They let me out of jail. Do you think they're going to care that I'm parked in front of your house minding my own business? Think again. You don't have daddy's money to save you anymore, and the police don't just help someone for the hell of it." Lenny makes a show of looking between Pax and Ferris and smirking. "I see you found a couple of guys to tag team. Wish I would have known you were this adventurous when we were together. It would have made things way more interesting." He releases a sinister chuckle, and Ferris is on him before Lenny realizes he moved. Ferris has him by the collar shoving him against his fancy car.

"Don't disrespect her like that. In fact, don't say anything to her. You need to get lost. She'll call the Sheriff to tell them you're stalking her."

"I don't give a fuck. I just need to talk to her. No one is going to arrest me for stalking anyone. I didn't do anything. I just came by to have a friendly chat with my ex-wife."

"Then you started running your mouth. I just met you, and I've already had enough. I can't imagine after being married to you she doesn't feel the same. Now climb your ass back into your car and roll on out. You aren't welcome here."

"Fuck you. I need to talk to her, and some skinny little pussy like you isn't going to send me on my way." I can tell Lenny's choice of words were the wrong ones as soon as Paxton closes the distance between him and his brother until he's right at his back. His posture straightens even more, and he looks somehow bigger than he did a second ago.

I can't see my ex, but I know by the stutter in his words that he's nervous. He can only pretend for so long before it becomes painfully obvious. "You, you, you, know what? F-f-f-f-fuck you. You can't always ha-ha-have her back. I'll g-g-et the answers I need when you two are gone. And you will be g-g-g-gone, she can't hold a man, much less two. Doesn't have the skill if you know what I mean." He chuckles in an uncomfortable way and wiggles away from Ferris. He gets into his car, starts it and speeds away with all of us watching him silently.

Finally, Ferris turns toward me. "You okay?"

I nod, though I'm not really. I'm exhausted, and I'm

ready to be in bed for a week. My old life is rearing its ugly head, as if I needed a reminder of what a mess it is. I mean I come home from a waitress job to a crappy little rental and to a dad who may or may not remember me—I didn't need any more reminders. Especially ones that will cost me money or time. My tires are going to be an expense that will cut close for us, but my ex popping back up is an annoyance I can't deal with. I didn't think I'd ever have to see him again. I have no idea why he's here. But I do know he won't go away until he gets whatever it is he wants. I'm just too tired to figure it out tonight.

"Thank you guys so much for your help. I'm sorry your tires got slashed because of my crap. You and Nick don't deserve it. You both are obviously good guys. I'll pay for the tires since it was my problem that got them slashed."

"Don't worry about that. I'm not. I'm more concerned about them making more trouble now that they know where you work and what you drive. Anger like that doesn't usually fizzle out after one little outburst."

"I'll be fine. Hopefully they'll go back to Ocala and leave me alone. If they don't, I'll deal with it. I've been dealing with all of this for a while, I just didn't think it would follow me here."

"I'm going to give you my number and if you have any more problems with them call me. If it's like this or worse call 911. Same with your ex. There's no reason for him to be lying in wait for you when you come home from work in the middle of the night, especially with the attitude he had. If you see him parked outside your place, keep driving. Don't stop and give him the chance to confront you. Call me."

Ferris holds out his hand waiting for me to place my cell phone in it. I'm reluctant. I don't want to burden anyone else with my problems, but I also don't want to rely on another man. I relied on my dad for years and then jumped right into relying on my ex. I don't want that to be the story of my life. I've relied on other people, and I never learned to take care of myself. I can really only trust myself. If Lenny taught me nothing else, he taught me that. Ferris must see the indecision on my face under the streetlights because he leans forward and pulls the phone out of my hand.

"I get why you would be skeptical about giving some guy you just met your number, but I think I've proven I don't want to harm you. I only want to help. I'm going to program Pax's number in here too. You can call him if you prefer, but you need to have someone who can help you. We don't mind. Think of your dad and how this could affect him."

I sigh. He's right. I can handle whatever they send my way, but my dad can't. And if someone hurts me, I won't be there to take care of him.

"Okay. I won't call unless it's an emergency though. I don't want to interrupt your lives for my craziness."

"Don't worry about that. Just be safe and call if you need us," he says as he squeezes my shoulder lightly and steps back. "We will wait here while you go inside and be by in the morning to drop off your car."

My heart melts a little. Such a nice guy. He saved me in more ways than one tonight, and I can't help but swoon a little inside. *Stop it!* I tell myself. I need to be swooning over a man like I need a slap across the face. I need to be strong and handle things myself and not get all mushy over a guy, especially one who isn't my type.

Keep going girl. Don't get distracted.

Until tonight things were going so much better. Sure, Dad's health was declining, but overall things have been good.

"Thank you so much for everything," I tell both of them,

meaning it more than they'd ever be able to understand. "I'll be careful, and I'll call if anything comes up. I appreciate your help getting my car taken care of. Tell Old Homer I'll drop by before work to pay for everything. Thanks again." I toss out as I turn and head for the house.

I don't want to stand out here any longer and see the pity on their faces or the burning need to help. They're good guys who don't need to end up in the middle of my drama. I give them one last wave as I enter the house and pray my dad is already asleep.

7

FERRIS

Something about the look on her face as she turned to go told me she wouldn't call us if something came up. I just met her. She has no reason to reach out to me, to trust that I'll take care of her. I have no claim over her, no ties to her, but something in me desperately wants to help her, to save her from the shit swirling around her. I have a history of that. It's my biggest fault. Trying to save drowning women, so to speak.

My last girlfriend was a stripper named Christy with a young son. She was pretty, she was sweet, and she was in need of help. Apparently, that's cat nip for a guy like me.

When I finally figured out Christy didn't want to be helped, realized she kept spending money on ridiculous unnecessary items, coming up short for bills, and partying a little too hard when she had to take care of her son the next day were poor choices I couldn't condone. I finally wised up and walked away. I may be a sucker for a woman in need, but I have enough self-respect to walk away when it's time.

It took me a few years, but I finally understand I'm a catch. I'm about to be making good money, I'm intelligent, in good physical shape, I have manners, a great family, and I do fit in that good-looking nerd category with my glasses. I have found most women I'm attracted to are attracted to guys like my brother Pax—big, badass looking dudes. Although I can drop a guy three times my size and paralyze him, most people underestimate me, especially women. I guess that comes with the teddy bear persona. Something I've always had. As far as Toni goes, I gave her the phone numbers, I'll take care of her car in the morning, and I'll go back to my job hunt.

When Pax and I get back to his house I grab my phone and sit in one of the rocking chairs on the front porch and pull up Chance's number. It's late even with the three hour time difference, but I just need to talk to him. He's probably the only one that will understand.

"Hey, mate! Everything okay?" Chance's accent makes me smile.

"I'm sorry it's so late. I just need to talk something out with you. There's a waitress at one of the restaurants in town that I met. We're just friends."

"Okay," he draws the word out like he's waiting for me to tell him more.

"She's got a little trouble. Her ex-husband is a real piece of work. It's a long story but I met him tonight and I think he's dangerous. I get the feeling that he's capable of doing anything to get what he wants."

"Do you care about this woman?"

"I just met her. I don't really know her. If I was staying here permanently I might try to get to know her better, but she comes with a ton of baggage from what I can tell. But that's not the point. Her ex is trouble with a capital T and I'm worried about her. She's sweet, seems to work hard and takes care of her sick father. I don't think she has any kind of support system. No family and no friends that I know of. Do you think it's stupid for me to get involved?"

"That's a loaded question, If you don't know this girl and don't have any kind of future with this girl it's probably best to walk away. If the ex is as bad as you think he might be, things aren't going to get better anytime soon." He pauses and I'm about to argue a different angle when he continues. "But, I know you mate. Number one. If someone needs help, you're going to jump in. It's just your nature. Number two if you weren't interested in her this wouldn't be a conversation. It's been a long time since you've even mentioned a woman in passing. Could this cause you a shit-ton of trouble? Yes. Should you run the other way? Probably. Are you going to? No. I know you mate, we're cut from the same cloth, and no matter what I say on this phone call you're going to help her. The only question I have is, is this girl worth going to jail for? I can't answer that for you. Only you can. My sister was, but she's family, so there was no question really. I'm not saying you'll end up in jail over whatever this is, but be prepared for the worst and know that's a possibility. I don't want you to bugger up the rest of your life without thinking about it first."

Chance went to prison for two years after beating the shit out of a drug addict who raped his sister. The whole situation was a mess, but I know Chance would do it all over again if given an option. He's right about me though. I don't know why I called him. I'll help Toni no matter what the outcome is, and it's not just because I'm fascinated by and attracted to her. I loathe bullies and I always pull for the underdog. With everything going on in Toni's life, she certainly qualifies as such.

～

THE NEXT DAY I'm sitting at Old Homer's shop waiting for him to wash the grease off his hands so we can settle the bill, and he can give me Toni's car when my cell phone rings. I look at the caller ID and smile. It's Chance. "Hey man, what's up? Sorry I called so late." I greet my friend as I pick up the phone.

"It's no big deal. You okay?"

"Yeah, I'm just picking up her car now and getting ready to take it to her."

He chuckles. "So you're going to help?"

"What do you think?" I smile at how well he knows me.

"I get it. I talked to Aubrey this morning and I want to know if your ready for your bike? She has a week off, and we thought we'd ride it out to you. We could use a change of scenery."

"Two thousand miles isn't a change of scenery. It's a life change. You don't need to come to Florida because of what's going on. In fact, you should stay as far away from this as possible. Things are going too good for you and Aubrey to worry about this. I can fly out there and get it if you're ready for it to be gone."

"Nah, mate. Seriously, we want to head out that way, and you know how much I love having that woman on the back of a bike."

"Seriou—" I interrupt.

"We want to make the trip. Do you want the bike or not?"

"Well, I'm not going to argue if you really want to. Having the bike would be great. I haven't accepted a job yet, but I'm sure I can park it at my brother's house until I find the place I want to be."

"We were talking about leaving next week, and it will take us a couple of days. We're probably going to do a little sightseeing during the trip. What's the best place to catch a return flight?"

"We're close to Tampa and Orlando airports, but Orlando is a zoo. I recommend Tampa."

"Great. See you soon. You're a good friend. Thanks." I smile as I say goodbye and hang up.

Hopefully, things with Toni will be settled down by the time they get here and there won't be anything to worry about. It will be awesome to see them. After the trip to California where I met them, I took a couple more trips to see them over the next two years, and they came up to Wyoming once. When I decided to get out of the Air Force, I told him I wanted to sell my bike and asked what I should get for it. He talked me out of it and said he and Aubrey would hold on to it while I was getting settled. Said it would give them an excuse to come out and see me. I guess they're making good on that.

They say people come into our lives at certain times for a reason. Well, his reason for coming into mine was to point out the truth, Christy was never meant for me, and I needed to move on. I'm still not sure what I've done to improve his life, but his friendship has meant the world to me.

Old Homer squints as he eyeballs the papers in front of him. He runs his shop old school style. No computers, only handwritten, paper invoices smudged with grease. He punches a few buttons on the ancient cash register and looks up at me. "You sure you want to pay for all of these, boy? It ain't cheap." I figured that. Three tires on three cars and a midnight tow truck for all of them. Is it my job to take care of it? No, but I don't want Toni to worry about this stuff. She has her hands full as it is, and judging by her place last night, she doesn't have a ton of extra cash to handle this.

I nod as I reply. "Yeah, I got it." I hand him my credit card. "What's the damage?"

He responds by making a statement rather than giving me the total. "I heard yous in da Air Force."

"I just got out. I'm looking for a civilian job. I'm ready to put down roots somewhere, and the Air Force doesn't know anything about roots."

"Ain't dat da truth." He nods knowingly. "I was in da Air Force, Vietnam, back in the beginning. Jet engine mechanic. Soons as I could, I got out. Hated Vietnam, too far from home. But da Air Force helped me get started here so I can't complain too much." I listen because I'm trying to figure out why he's telling me this. I don't mind listening, as people tend to share their own military stories or tell you who they know and what branch they were in when they hear you served.

"They were good to me while I was in too."

He nods, and I notice the many lines in his old, dark face and wonder how old he is. In his seventies maybe?

"Well, pick up last night is on me. I like ta see a man takin' care of a woman, and I support a fellow airman doing jus dat. You don't look like much of a mechanic, but my eyes are gettin' bad, and I'm old so what do I know. Ya need a job? I can find something for ya to do."

"Thanks for the offer, but you're right, I'm not a mechanic. I'm a computer guy. I've got some interviews coming up. Something will pan out."

He coughs as he chuckles, probably a smoker. "Whas yo name?"

"Ferris, good to meet you." I reach out to shake his hand.

"Name's Henry, but everybody's call me Old Homer for's long as I can 'member, so jus call me dat."

"Good to meet you Old Homer and thanks for coming out last night."

"Ya total is $1002.32 cents."

"That can't be right. Should be much more."

"Nah. Thas the total. I told ya, pick up was on me. I also gave ya a military discount." I can't help but smile at the old man. This is something to love about a small town. People take care of people.

"I can't tell you how much I appreciate it."

"Jus come see me when ya need ya oil changed."

"Don't worry, I will." Before I turn to leave, I ask, "Hey, do you work on motorcycles?"

"Nah, my friend Charlie does though. I'll git ya his number when ya ready. Come back by and shoot da shit wit an ole man sometime."

"I can do that. Thanks again." I tell him as he hands me all three sets of car keys. I go out to the parking lot and start Toni's car. I can drop if off for her and then jog back up here. It's only about a mile, and I missed my run with Pax this morning to take care of this.

I drive over and pull into the driveway. Everything is quiet, and I hate to knock in case she's still asleep, but I'm not leaving her keys outside or in an unlocked car. I knock lightly and glance at my watch. It's nine o'clock. "Who is it?" Toni's voice calls out from the other side of the door, and I realize she doesn't have a peep hole. That's not safe especially with the shit she has going on.

"It's Ferris with your car keys." The lock turns with a click, and Toni stands in the doorway with her glasses on and her hair mussed. The satin pajama shorts set isn't doing much to hide her feminine curves, and I can't help but glance down. I feel like such a creeper, but damn she's beautiful in the morning.

My cheeks heat. What man blushes? Me obviously, looking at her. I hold out the keys to her before I utter a word, then I clear my throat and force myself not to glance back down at her bare legs and pert nipples poking into the shiny fabric. "Your car is out front. Old Homer changed your oil too, said the light was on and it was passed time. I'm taking Nick's up to the Lobster Lounge now.

"You didn't have to bring it to me. I was going to get it today. I need to get dressed and pay him."

"No need, he gave us a discount, and I took care of it earlier."

"A discount? Like a 3 for one special?" she jokes and the lightness in her voice takes me by surprise.

"Nah. A military discount. He saw my T-shirt this morning. Turns out he was in the Air Force back in the day."

"Oh, I see. Well then, I owe you. Let me grab my checkbook."

She turns to go when her dad comes around the corner with his walker. "Who's there, Toni?"

"Just a friend, Dad. Go sit down before you fall."

"Well invite him in," he says with a smile. They obviously aren't ready for the day judging by their appearances. Toni's pajamas and mussed hair are only outdone by his tufts of wild hair sticking out at the sides of his head while wearing his wife beater with plaid pajama pants.

"Dad, we aren't even dressed."

"We never have company. Come in, come in. I'm sure an old man in his PJ's won't scare him."

Grinning I move through the door and shut it behind me. "Nope, a dude in his Pj's won't scare me. It's nice to see you again sir." I reach out to shake his hand.

"We've met before?" His brow furrows.

"Yes, sir. When you were out berry picking with Toni. Don't worry it was a hot day, I would forget too."

"Oh, right, right, right," he mutters obviously not remembering, but too polite to let on.

Toni ushers her dad back to his recliner. "Have a seat, Dad. You can hang out with Ferris while I grab my checkbook."

"You don't need to do that. It was no big deal. I told you he gave me a discount."

She props her hands on her hips. "Discount doesn't mean free."

I ignore her and turn my attention to her dad. "So what do you have planned today?"

"I don't know. I just go where Toni tells me to, and she hasn't said what we're doing today."

Toni yells from somewhere down the hall. "I didn't know I was going to have a car, so I didn't make plans. Now we can go to the grocery store, we need a few things."

"Grocery store? Ugh. Let's go fishing. We can catch our food, just like when you were little."

"Dad, I have to work today. We can't go fishing. Besides, you can't get onto a boat right now. You aren't steady enough."

"We don't need a boat," he shouts down the hall to her. "We can fish from the riverbank."

The sound of her grumbling carries down the hall. I want to laugh at his persistence and her irritation, but I think that would only piss her off.

When she appears, she's in black spandex shorts and a woman's cut T-shirt. Her alabaster skin is stark against the black shorts, and I think about how soft the skin probably is, like satin on a cool evening.

Damn it, I need to stop.

"Come on, Toni. Take an old man fishing," he pleads with her.

"Dad, I have to work tonight, and we need food. This way I don't have to order out again."

I'm not sure what possesses me, but I blurt out, "I can take you fishing while she goes to the store."

Her mouth drops open before she recovers quickly. "I don't think—" she starts, but I cut her off.

"We'll be fine. Mike Wade, who came out last night, has a house on the river with a nice dock. We can go over there for a little bit while you go to the store. It's a win-win situation. I love to fish, but I'll find a job soon enough and won't be able to go in the middle of the day. Besides he really wants to. You can have some time to yourself."

She chews on her bottom lip. The indecision is killing her. She wants to say yes, but probably doesn't want to pawn her dad off on me. "Seriously, we'll be okay. Let me call Mike and make sure it's cool with him."

I dial Mike's number and explain I'd like to bring a friend fishing on his dock. When I hang up, I smile at her dad. "We're on. You have some breakfast and get dressed. I need to drop off Nick's car and pick up my rental before I'll be back to get you."

"I knew I liked you, son," her dad declares, and when I glance at her she's rolling her eyes. The good thing about this exchange is that she forgot all about the money. I stand and head back toward the door. "See you in about forty-five minutes to an hour." I don't give either of them time to reply. I slip out the door and jog back to Old Homer's place to do what I need to do.

An hour and fifteen minutes later, I'm seated next to Paul on the dock. We took our time so it took us a little while to walk from the car to the dock with his walker. Once we got to the dock he wanted to stand, but he's so unsteady on his feet I convinced him to sit down in a chair. The last thing we need is for him to end up in the river. I'd really be in trouble then. I doubt we'll catch anything, but it's not a bad way to spend a couple of hours. Scooter, the basset hound groans at my feet and stretches out. I shift the fishing pole to my other hand and reach down to scratch his exposed belly. "That's a fat hound," Paul remarks. Mike met us back here when we first arrived to make sure we were set up, and Scooter refused to go back inside with him.

"Yeah, he's always been this way apparently. Mike got him at the pound a long time ago, and he was already plumped right up."

"Good dog, though."

"Yeah, he is. And he's great with their little girl too."

"Little girls will steal your heart," Paul says quietly.

"I bet. I don't have any kids to know that for sure."

"Little girls are the kryptonite of dads all over the world. There's nothing I wouldn't do for my Toni."

"You've taken good care of her, sir. She's a good woman."

"I'm too old to take care of her. She has to take care of me, and that just feels wrong. Someday you'll understand."

"Maybe someday I'll be lucky enough to have a family." That's what I want more than anything.

"Ah, you'll find the right one. I just hope you pick better than I did. My wife, Beulah, turned out to be a cheater. She ran away with the guy." It's interesting he remembers that today. It has to be frustrating going in and out of understanding.

"That had to be tough," I tell him.

"It was, but some of it was probably my fault. I worked too much. Didn't pay attention to her, or not as much as I should have. Though she never complained. One day she just cleaned out our savings account and took off with the guy. It hurt Toni as much as me because she didn't even look back to say goodbye to her daughter. Granted, Toni was an adult, but as far as I know she hasn't heard from her since then. I had to hire a private investigator to find her so I could serve her the divorce papers. She was just going to start a new life somewhere without ending her old one."

There is only one thing to say to that information. "That sucks."

"Yes, it does."

We sit quietly for a while until he finally gets a bite. My hook is still not producing any action, so I stand to lean over the dock and watch as he reels in a catfish that's probably about fourteen or fifteen inches long. I hold the end of the line and unhook the fish. He grins from ear to ear, so proud he caught something. Catfish caught in the bay are not something you keep and eat so I hand it to him. He holds it awkwardly as I pull out my phone and snap a quick picture. I take the fish from him and toss it back into the water. His smile doesn't fade so I bait his hook and move so he can cast again.

After a couple of hours, he's caught a few small red snapper and a couple more catfish. I only caught one small catfish. We throw them all back, but I can tell just by the grin he wears the whole morning he's enjoying himself, and I'm glad I took the time to spend with him this morning.

The growl of his stomach alerts me to the time. A quick glance at my watch shows it's 12:30 "You ready to eat?" I stand and reel in my line.

"Yeah, I could go for a little something."

"Okay, let me call Toni and let her know we're stopping to eat before we go home."

I'm thankful she gave me her number when her dad

came with me. I dial her number, and she picks up on the first ring, her voice anxious. "Is everything okay?"

"Well, hello to you too. Everything is fine. It's getting too hot, and we're hungry. Do you care if I take your dad to lunch?" It's quiet on the other end of the line for a little too long.

"Hello? Toni? Are you there?"

She clears her throat and answers. "Yeah, yes. Sorry. I... I..."

"Hey, it's okay. He's fine. It's just lunch. It'll give you some more time for yourself unless you want to meet us. I'm sure you have to be hungry too. It's up to you. I can handle this if you want time, otherwise meet us at Waterfront Social in about fifteen minutes."

"Oh, okay," her voice is soft. "Thank you. You're so thoughtful."

"It's nothing. I'm enjoying it."

"Okay," I can hear a smile in her voice.

I say goodbye and disconnect.

I gather our fishing poles and empty drink containers and follow Paul to the house. I lift my hand to knock on the door when it flies open. Sarah stands in the doorway with a popsicle in one hand and a grin on her face that's framed with a wild mop of blonde hair. Her mom walks up right behind her and pushes the screen door open for us. "Come on in guys." Summer smiles at us and moves out of the way. Paul makes his way through the door using his walker, and Scooter follows right behind him.

"Thanks for letting us use your dock and your dog," I say as I slide past them all and carry the fishing poles to the garage.

When I come back I hear Paul telling Summer how she looks like a movie star. I'm not sure if I should tell him that she is a movie star, or if I should just let him think he's flattering a pretty lady. I decide to stay quiet and let him have his flirty moment.

"Come on, Casanova. We need to eat lunch. I'm starved."

"I ate all my peanut butter and jelly, so I got a popsicle," Sarah informs us proudly.

"That's a great treat. You're so lucky," I inform her as I ruffle her hair.

"Next time I'll bring you one." Her little grin is infectious.

"Thanks, kiddo. I look forward to it."

We say our goodbyes, and I help Paul out to the car. We drive the short distance to the little waterfront restaurant, and when we arrive Toni is waiting for us on the walkway to the dock. Once we're seated and have placed our order, her dad tells her everything about our fishing trip, and I'm glad that he can remember. After Toni confirmed my suspicions this morning about Paul's dementia, I was afraid that as soon as we got in the car this afternoon and drove away, he would forget our little fishing trip and the happiness he felt for a short time. He was so lucid while we were on the dock it's easy to forget that he may not remember after today. For now, though, he's able to share his joy with Toni who is grinning from ear to ear as she listens to his description of our morning.

This restaurant has a little seating area inside, but the best seat in the house is on the covered patio out back that overlooks Crystal River. The fans above us circulate the warm air efficiently, and although it's probably too hot to be outside for lunch this time a year, the view is too good to waste by eating inside. The river gently rolls by here, and if you're lucky the manatee feed on the grass along the seawall or the dolphin swim by in their pods. The food is above average, and the staff is all courteous and efficient. It would be a great place to bring a date. We could've gone to one of the sports bars close by or a chain restaurant, but I figured since he doesn't get out much and obviously enjoys the outdoors, this is probably the best place. Now that Toni's here, I'm very glad I chose this location.

"I haven't been here before." Her voice is quiet and wistful, her eyes are soft as she takes in the scenery.

"I came here with my parents when I first got home. My mom loves it."

"What are your parents like?" she asks as her dad stares out at the water seemingly content.

"The best people I know. Strong and kind, tough but nurturing, and supportive in every way."

"They sound perfect."

"Close to it." I don't share more because I'm not sure if she really cares or is just making polite conversation.

"Do you have any brothers or sisters? You seem to be handling things well on your own." I nod toward her dad, so I don't say it out loud and make him feel bad.

"Nope. I'm an only child. My grandparents have been gone for ten years, and my aunt got married and moved to Washington State when she was young and never looked back. So it's just us. I don't mind. We're tight. Aren't we, Dad?" She reaches over and pats his hand, pulling his attention from the water.

With a gentle smile he asks, "What did you say, honey?"

"That we're a team. We take care of each other, right?"

"Always." Is his answer. I'm glad they share their feelings, but I also get how hard it must be for her at times. His memory is so finicky. It comes and goes on a whim.

Conversation is light but intelligent through our meal, and I realize how much I miss having conversations with a woman. Her dad stays quiet for the most part. He doesn't eat as much food as Toni would like, and I make a mental note to google Dementia because I have a feeling his little appetite has something to do with it. He seemed so hungry when we left Mike's house.

When the meal is over, I walk them to her car. "I'll be glad to take him fishing again when I get back from my interviews this week. I have one on Tuesday and one on Thursday, but after that I have a few days. I'll check in with you to see if he's up for it."

"You don't have to do that. He rarely remembers that he likes to fish. I'm wondering if he remembers he was fishing this morning."

"As long as he's not combative I don't mind taking him, even if he forgets he was there ten minutes later. It was relaxing, and it made him happy. Plus, it might give you some time to yourself that you don't usually get." I shrug like it's no big deal, but I'm really hoping she'll say yes. I want to help this woman. I want to do things that bring that small, sweet smile to her face. And it's not just because I have this whole savior complex. I like her and want to make her happy. I doubt she has a lot of happy moments.

"Okay, well, we can see how he's doing later in the week. Thank you so much for taking him and for buying us lunch. I wish you wouldn't have, especially since you just took care my car."

"It was nothing. It was a nice change, and I'm glad I could take a pretty girl and her dad to lunch." One side of her mouth ticks up, and her eyes sparkle. She's wearing contacts today, and it's easier to see her green eyes. I lean in and kiss her cheek and then shake her dad's hand.

"Thanks again."

I turn and walk toward my rental car and do my best not to turn around to see her one more time.

That evening at dinner the topic of conversation is Toni. My brother, being always observant, noticed my growing interest in Toni. "Do you think you should get involved with someone who has so much baggage? I looked into her, and she is knee-deep in some shit. I emailed you links to the articles."

"Dude." It's a one-word warning.

"I'm just looking out for you. Do me a favor and just check it out, for me. I want your eyes wide open. Also, what if you start something with her and then take a job in Miami or Jacksonville? How's that gonna work?"

"I'm not starting anything with her. I barely even know her," I protest, but even I can admit, in my head, I've thought of that. My brother is seeing things in me I thought I was keeping concealed.

"Bullshit."

"Paxton." My sister-in-law groans. "I don't want our kids using that language."

"Sorry." He has the decency to at least look apologetic. "I saw the way you held her. You took her dad fishing today for God's sake and then took them to lunch. I bet if I call Old Homer, he'll tell me you paid for her car to be fixed."

My eyes shift from his to Shay and back, not wanting him to see the truth.

"Damn it. She's gonna use you."

"She hasn't asked me for anything. I just see someone in need and want to help. It's not hurting anyone, least of all me."

"I'm pretty sure we had this same conversation when you got together with Christy."

"I knew you were going to bring that up. This is not the

same thing. I just want to help her. Chill. I'm a grown ass man. I can take care of myself."

"I get that, but I'm your brother, and it's my job to make sure you're okay. I don't care how old we get, that will always be my job."

"I know, and I appreciate it, but it's something I need to do. It's something she needs me to do, she just doesn't know it. I don't care if nothing ever develops, I'm in a position where I can help someone so I will. Let me do what I need to do."

He studies me closely for a moment. "Fine. Let me know if you need anything."

"Thanks, bro."

He waves his hand at me like it's no big deal. I decide I'm going to Lobster Lounge after dinner to make sure her car is okay, and no one is harassing her. I mean, why not?

8

TONI

Ferris took my dad fishing and then both of us to lunch. I sit and ponder that as the television plays an old rerun of Ponderosa for my dad. It was a nice lunch too, and I don't just mean the food. I enjoyed his conversation, even if it was mostly surface stuff. He seemed to sense we couldn't go too deep with my dad around, and he didn't push. I couldn't help but notice, and not for the first time, that he's handsome. He doesn't have that knock you out of your socks at first sight look like Paxton, but he's got the most crystalline blue eyes that get little crinkles around them when he smiles. Seriously, those eyes, I wish I could explain it, there's just something about them that intrigues me.

Not to mention those perfect lips. All through lunch I wanted to touch them to see if they felt as soft as they look. And his voice. Good Lord, his voice is deep, but quiet and soothing. I love it.

The last thing I need to be thinking about is a man, especially one I don't know well, but I can't seem to help it.

My thoughts keep drifting back to the Lobster Lounge when he kicked those people out, or when he settled me down and took care of business when we found all of our tires slashed. Then today when he was so sweet and patient with my dad and tried to give me time to myself. It penetrated some of the armor I've built around myself. I tried to ignore it and just let it go as someone being nice to us, but it really got to me in a way that nothing has in a long time or maybe even ever.

As I drive to work, I think about what it would be like to date a man like him and have a normal life. One without crazy disgruntled ex-employee confrontations, the negative stigma of my family name, and a dad with dementia. Luckily the drive to work is short, so I don't have more time to think about what I'm missing. Today is a day I wish my life was ordinary.

Business is slow until about seven o'clock, so I spend time rolling extra silverware and helping with the dishes.

When it picks up, I lose myself in taking care of my customers and somehow miss when Ferris takes a seat at the bar. By the time I spot him, I'm halfway to the bar to order a round of beer for one of my tables. I have no idea how long he's been here, and butterflies begin to swarm in my belly. A spike of excitement courses through me that he might be here to see me. I should probably find it creepy that he's here after seeing him already today and last night, but I don't. It makes me almost giddy.

I stop at the end of the bar and give my order to Nick before I turn toward him with a goofy grin. "Hey stranger, long time no see."

"Sorry, I'm not trying to stalk you, but I was just worried you might have more trouble tonight."

"You don't need to worry about me, I'll be okay," I tell him, and although I don't doubt that I will be okay, I'm hoping he sticks around anyway.

"Well, I'll just be here to make sure. I realize you're tough enough to handle all these things, I just don't think you should have to do it alone."

My smile is genuine, and I quickly glance over at Nick who I can tell has been listening but has been making drinks farther down the bar. He's smiling his approval to me. My chest warms, and I lay my hand on Ferris's arm softly. "Thank you. It means a lot."

His good ole boy grin returns along with those little crinkles by his eyes. I have the sudden urge to take off his glasses and stare at his eyes without anything in the way.

"No problem," he answers, breaking me out of my lust filled stupor.

"I have to go get the rest of their order and put it in. I'll stop back by when I have a minute."

"Don't worry, I'm fine right here."

The rest of the night goes by in a blur of customers and clean up, and before I know it Mr. Clark—the owner of the Lobster Lounge— is telling me I can go. My feet ache, but my heart is light, and I'm a little nervous. Ferris has waited for me and plans to follow me home to make sure there are no issues. How sweet is that? I'm sure he has better things to do than sit here playing sentry all night and escorting me home.

With a warm hand on my lower back, he leads me out of the restaurant toward my car which I parked right under one of the parking lot lights. I'm not sure how much of a deterrent it is for someone wanting to mess with it tonight, but I don't want to make things any easier for vandals.

When we reach my car, I pause and turn around, resting my weight against my car and look up at him. My heart is racing, and I'm a little nervous, but I have to know if he's just some do-gooder kind of guy who sees someone in need and jumps in or if he's maybe interested in me. My gut says he's interested, but it's been a long time since my intuition has been accurate about anything.

"Why did you really come here tonight?" He opens his mouth to respond, and I continue, "Are you here because you just like taking care of people in general, or are you here because you're interested in me? I can't get a read on you and can't understand why you would give up your time for me."

He stares at me in a thoughtful way, like he's trying to sort out his words. I get the feeling he's not an impulsive man. "Well, to be honest, I would help anyone who I thought needed it. I'm that kind of person."

My cheeks heat a little with embarrassment that I would even think a good guy like him would be interested in me in any kind of romantic or sexual way. My eyes shift from his face to the ground, and I wish I would have just gotten in my car and pulled away. Now I'm not sure how to get out of this situation without making it more awkward than I already have.

"But there's something about you that draws me in. I've been thinking about you since we sat in your section that first night we were introduced. You invading my thoughts has only gotten worse with each time I've seen you since. The fact that circumstances have dictated you needing assistance has just given me an excuse to get closer to you and try to get to know you."

The embarrassment recedes as quick as it washed over me, and a new feeling, a warm one filled with a buzz of happiness, flows inside me. His head cocks to the side a little as he studies my reaction, and he must like what he sees because he slowly closes the distance between us, lifts his hand and brushes my long bangs away from my glasses and tucks a stray piece of hair behind my ear. His touch is gentle but deliberate as his fingers trace the line of my jaw, stopping at my chin and tilting it up.

"You can say no, but I've been dying to kiss you since you licked your lips after you guzzled that water in my brother's living room." He's so close I can feel his words whisper across my lips. "Is this okay?"

Every nerve ending in my body is alive and fired up. How can you get turned on from a few words and a sweet touch while standing in a parking lot? I don't know the answer to that question, but I do know it's happening. I nod slightly, unable to form words, and he closes the distance.

His kiss is gentle and sweet, but also somehow hot and exciting. I've never had a closed mouth kiss that moved me like this one. He pulls back slightly but stays painfully close. "Was that okay?" The heat of his words tumble together with my suddenly raging hormones, and I nod again. "Good, because I'm not done." His hand slides back along my jaw and his fingers filter into my hair as he cups my head and brings my mouth to his, this time his lips are slightly parted and his tongue snakes out to trace my lips. A tiny whimper escapes, and I open for him, my brain screaming the invitation for him to come inside. God, have I ever had a kiss like this? The answer is absolutely not. I've never been this lucky.

I finally snap out of the la la land I've been in since he leaned into me and slip my hands up his shirt until I reach the skin at his waist and continue around to his back. His muscles flex under my fingers, and I get a sudden flash of him jogging shirtless past me when we were blackberry picking. All of those muscles he keeps hidden under his clothes are like nothing I've ever touched before. Steel covered in smooth skin. The kiss grows hungrier as my hands caress his back and sides while his fingers grip my hair. His other hand snakes around my waist to pull me closer. Dear God, I can feel his growing erection between us as we continue making out like teenagers. It should probably freak me out he's this turned on by a kiss, but honestly, so am I.

His mouth is passionate, hungry, confident, and everything I ever fantasized about. My nails dig into his skin, and I'm ready to hike a leg up and grind against him to bring some relief to my aching core when several voices coming from the entrance of the building bring us back to reality. He pulls back just enough to settle things down a notch and rests his forehead against mine.

"I'm sorry. I took that too far," he confesses, breathless. His eyes stay closed, his forehead still against mine, his breath, heavy like we were running a race.

"No, don't apologize. I didn't want it to end."

"Are you in a hurry to get home? I realize they cut you out of there a little early tonight."

"Not really. Gigi, the lady who stays with my dad always tries to get me to stay out later after work. Why?"

"I'd like to take you some place. It's not fancy, but the moon is full, and the sky is clear, it should be perfect."

"Sounds nice. Should I change clothes? I don't have anything with me."

"No, what you're wearing is fine."

He pulls his phone out of his pocket and sends a text. A moment later his phone dings quietly, and he glances at it and grins. "Okay, we're all set. Follow me so we don't have to worry about leaving your car here in case someone decides to be a jerk again. It's less than five minutes from here."

I follow him past the main street in Crystal River into a small neighborhood by King's Bay. We pull up to a beautiful ranch style house and get out of our cars. He strides toward me, and it's only when he gets close that I see the big smile. He reaches out and grabs my hand and pulls me gently toward the back yard. "Come on. This is Mike Wade's house, the guy who came out to help us last night. The same place I took your dad fishing. I asked if we could come use their dock, and he said yes. Although Scooter will be out here to chaperone us."

"Um, who's Scooter?" I ask, wondering why two grown adults need a chaperone.

"You'll see." His cryptic message has a hint of humor laced in it.

Once we get around to the backyard, I realize why he brought me here. It's beautiful and romantic with the way the moon is full and hanging low in the sky reflecting off the water. The crickets are singing their summer song and little flickers of light from the lightning bugs are flashing all over the yard. The back door opens as we reach the deck, and Mike from the other night sticks his head out. "Hey guys! Y'all need anything to drink?"

"I'm fine. You need anything Toni?"

"No but thank you."

"Okay, just knock if you need something, or if you are ready to send Scooter back in."

"No problem and thanks again, Mike. We appreciate it." He lifts his chin, and before he can shut the door a short, round dog with ears long enough to trip over trots out toward us. Ferris squats down and rubs the hefty, little dog down, cooing sweet words to him like one would a baby or a little kid.

"Toni, meet Scooter, Mike and Summer's Bassett hound. If they didn't let him out, he would bark or howl the whole time. We're buddies, he likes to hang out with me."

I bend down to stroke his soft fur and scratch behind his ears. "It's nice to meet you, Scooter." I turn to Ferris. "He howls?"

"Oh yeah, it's the saddest and most annoying sound you've ever heard. So when I'm around, I let Scooter hang out with me. He loves being outside when people are in the backyard. Your dad got to hang out with him when we were fishing."

"It's a nice spot. I bet my dad loved it," I say, my voice wistful and a little sad. He has always loved the outdoors. Fishing, hunting, horseback riding.

"That's why I want to bring him back. Even if he doesn't remember it later, at least he can experience it in the moment. He really was content and even happy."

"Thank you, it was sweet of you."

"I'm a sweet guy." This time his grin is wolfish, almost cocky and a little playful. Not a side of Ferris I've seen much of.

I stand up and bump him with my shoulder, the little bit of flirtation warms my soul. It's been too long since someone has flirted with me.

He wraps his arm around me and leads me to a bench swing in a wooden A-frame stand that faces the water. Before we sit, he leans down and picks the dog up. Ferris's arm wraps around me and pulls me in close on his left side while Scooter rests his head on Ferris's lap. My feet dangle and he pushes us back gently, his long legs able to keep us going.

"This is really nice." I sigh.

"I thought you could use a little bit of peace."

"This place fits the bill. Thank you." I lean my head against him, and I feel his lips press against my hair. Also, nice. Comforting in a way I not only want but also need.

We sit quietly for a long time, gently swinging. The song of the crickets and bullfrogs fill the night air, along with the occasional snores from the sleeping dog next to Ferris. Is there a better place to be? A more perfect moment? I'd say no, at least not for me.

"You probably need to get home, don't you?"

"Unfortunately, yeah. Gigi wouldn't mind, but I don't want to take advantage of her. She's so good to us."

"Let me get Scooter inside, and we can go."

I stand before he can and step over to where the dog is stretched out next to him. Scooter's eyes are open. He's watching me but hasn't moved yet. My fingers glide across his silky fur. "You're such a good boy. Are you always this sweet?" I croon at the relaxed pooch.

"I want a dog like him when I get settled somewhere. Hudson and Stacey have a couple of energetic dogs. They're cute but rowdy. I need one more like this. A chill kind of guy."

"You do seem pretty laid back."

"I am. I always have been, even before my parents died."

A sliver of ice slides down my spine. "Your parents died?" My heart hurts for him.

"Those are my adoptive parents. My parents and my little sister died in a house fire while I was spending the night with friends when I was young. I didn't move in with the Pearsal's until I was almost fifteen."

My hand rubs my chest to soothe the instant pain that spreads at hearing his news. My stomach rolls over at the thought of Ferris as a little kid finding out that his whole family and way of life are gone when he's been at a sleepover. My life has been in a downward spiral for a while, but at least I'm an adult. At least I still have my dad.

My voice is quiet as I run my fingers across his jaw soothingly. "I'm so sorry. That's horrible."

"It is, but it was a long time ago. I don't talk about it, ever." Our eyes hold for a long time. It's a strangely intimate moment for both of us, being completely clothed and nothing physical going on. His pain is still palpable even after all this time, but he's obviously good at hiding it. His life hasn't been easy either.

The thoughts and concerns about my crappy situation in life that usually run through my head have been silent the whole time we've been out here, but something about this intimate moment starts them rolling around in my head again. I have no business being out here in the moonlight like this with any man, much less one who's probably not sticking around. One who has so much potential to be more to me. I don't have time in my life for a distraction of this magnitude. I need to work, save money, spend time with and care for my dad. There's no room for sweet, obviously romantic men who are going to leave soon. That's a headache and heartache I don't want to have. I swallow hard and lower my hand, trying to put some distance between us again. What was I thinking coming out here like this?

Ferris studies my face for a long moment, and I wonder if he notices the distance I put between us. It's a weird feeling, almost as if he can read my thoughts. "Come on, let's get you home." He stands, and I back up as he lowers Scooter to the ground so he can trot back to the house.

By the time we get Scooter inside and are standing out front, my body is feeling the late hour and the long day. I should fall asleep easy tonight if I can shut off the little hamster on the wheel that is my brain right now. "Thank you for a really nice night. I needed this." I try to be gracious because he was trying to do something nice for me. Ferris is kind, he's hot, he's smart, and he's thoughtful. I just don't need a guy right now especially one who is only here temporarily.

His hand slides under my hair around my neck, and he steps in close to me. "You're welcome. I'm glad I could help." I squirm a little because I just talked myself out of anything further with Ferris, and here he is, holding me so tenderly my body is melting right into him.

My brain argues with my body, telling me not to let this go any further. My body ignores the warnings and literally turns to putty with his touch. My mouth stays quiet, unsure of what I'll say if I open it. I need to stop this, but I know what his lips feel like, and I don't want to stop it. Maybe a little kiss won't hurt? He leans in and presses his lips to mine gently. His mouth... good God. I mean seriously, what man has lips that soft? He pulls away briefly before he dives back in, deeper this time. My body overrides my mind completely, flooding it with hormones so it's foggy as hell. I act on instinct, sliding my hands up under his shirt, and as soon as my hands make contact with his lean muscled body I ignite. I can't help myself. Before long I'm pressed against the side of my car, and we are making out like teenagers again. We're all lips, tongues, hands and heaving breaths. Finally, he's the one to slow it down and bring it to a stop. With his forehead resting against mine, our breath mingles as we try to slow our heart rates.

"Can I take you out on your next day or night off? On a real date?"

The brain fog brought on by the rush of hormones keep

me from saying a very firm no. I should walk away. Except that's not an option at this point. Apparently, my now awake-and-paying-attention libido isn't interested in being a bitch. "I don't know if that's a good idea. My life is a train wreck, and you're probably moving out of the area as soon as you can."

"Your life being a train wreck is even more reason for you to say yes. A little fun will do you some good. As for me leaving, I don't know when that will be yet. I'm still interviewing so let's not get ahead of ourselves. Just say yes. I'll pay for Gigi to stay with your dad so you don't take a financial hit when you go out with me."

I fight a smile. He knew what my next excuse was going to be. Damn it. Why does a guy who is so obviously perfect have to come along at the absolute worst time for both of us?

He's not deterred by my indecision. "I can tell you want to go. Just tell me what day and we will work everything out."

He's probably right. I should do something enjoyable without worry of the future or all the crap that has been and still could go wrong. "My next day off is Tuesday. Let me talk to Gigi and make sure she can stay with my dad." The smile he graces me with when he gets the answer he was working for is worth the yes, even though I know it's going to end badly.

This time, when our lips connect, the kiss is deep, slow, and powerful. The feel of his hand on the back of my neck and the one snaking around my waist sends chills up my arms and down my legs. The subtle tilt of his head as he changes direction of the kiss and the increasing intensity make this moment indescribable. This kiss is commanding, sexy, absolutely amazing. I'm not sure I've experienced this kind of intensity with someone before. God, he's strong, confident, and exerts enough control to hold you together before you come apart at the seams with want, without taking over the moment completely. It's the best kiss I've ever had, even beating out the ones from earlier in the evening.

9

FERRIS

My drive to Miami the next day seems to take forever. The traffic in south Florida is ridiculous, especially after living in Wyoming for the last few years and then staying in Crystal River the last couple of weeks. The slow pace of those places makes this look like a kicked beehive. My arrival at the corporate headquarters for Sonavive Tech was not what I was expecting. I push through the double doors of the mirrored high rise building and am greeted by a security guard who explains that I have to go through the security checkpoint and then into a room off to the side to get a visitor's badge. Thank goodness I arrived early, or I would have been late.

By the time I get all the way through security and up to the thirty-third floor, I'm frustrated. The secretary guard seated inside the suite door stands and announces to me and the other nine or ten people waiting that we will start with a group interview in the conference room before we take turns in one-on-one and paneled interviews. It would have helped if the man I've spoken with up to this point regarding the interview would have explained how they do things. I could have been better prepared. I do my best work one-on-one. A group interview is the kiss of death for a guy like me. Luckily, by the look of the other people filing into the conference room they are just as blindsided as I am.

By the time I finish the three-hour interview process I'm irritable and ready for a beer. I dial Dev's number and wait for him to pick up. "Hey man! Been waiting forever. You ready to grab a bite to eat?" Dev asks by way of greeting.

"Yeah, man. It's been a long day. Lucianna gonna meet us?"

"I think you killed enough time that she can get away. I'll shoot you the address to the restaurant so you don't have to fight traffic to our place."

We hang up, and I follow his instructions to a little Italian restaurant with a view of the water and find them already waiting for me. Dev is tall and relatively muscular, but leaner like me with reddish hair and Lucianna is short and curvy with dark brown hair. They're physical opposites but make a striking couple.

I kiss Lucianna's cheek and shake hands with Dev before we all sit down. "How did it go?" Of course, Lucianna, being the lawyer, fires off the first question.

"I'm not sure. It turned out to be a three-part interview. Group, panel, and one-on-one. I don't think I did great, but honestly, I'm not sure I care."

Dev sits back in his chair and signals for the server. "Why is that?"

The server appears, and we put in our drink orders before I answer. "No offense to you guys, but the traffic here sucks, and I didn't get a good feeling about that company or the process. I would just be another number there. I don't need to be the number one guy anywhere, but that place is so big that I could disappear and no one would notice for a few days. After my time in the Air Force, I'm not sure I want to be just another cog in the wheel."

"I get that. Did you not realize how big the company was before you interviewed?" Lucianna always asks the most direct questions.

"I did my research, I had an idea of the size of the company, but some companies are good about making small pockets in big organizations instead of capitalizing on the sheer enormity of the business. Sonavive Tech has no interest in taking things down a notch. They're big tech with big visions and want an army to complete all the tasks. That's just not what I'm looking for. I'm glad I gave it a shot, but I think even with an offer I won't take it."

"Where else are you interviewing?" Dev wants to know.

"I've got an interview later in the week in Jacksonville with a contractor who primarily works with the Navy. That one is a little more promising. The company is smaller and the person I've been communication with is the one who will actually interview me. I also have an interview in Tampa with a company who makes parts for communications equipment. The job itself doesn't seem that interesting, but I like the idea of being relatively close to my family." I shrug. "We'll see how things pan out. I had a few people reach out from California, Atlanta, and a company in St. Louis, but I don't want to be that far from family again. I got enough of that when I was in the service."

"I can relate. Have you talked to Mike Wade about working for Sunset Security? I know they started talking about hiring again."

"I'm not Paxton. That guy could drop a man with a twist of a wrist and a scary look. I can hold my own, but no one is going to look at me and feel safe with me providing security."

"We're branching out. Not just looking for field guys. We need techies too. Mike won't hire just anyone. I already know he likes you and taking a job with us would have you really close to family. Just think about it. Hell, talk to him. Let him know it's a possibility. I've never been happier, man."

He reaches over and grabs Lucianna's hand and squeezes.

"I doubt they are handing out Luciannas in their bene-fits packages," I joke. Lucianna is beautiful, smart, and can be sweet, but my interests are in a woman a little more docile than the fiery Latina across from me.

"No doubt, she makes life better, but as far as jobs go, you won't find a better boss or team than you will at Sunset. You'll have to find your own Lucianna though." He leans over and kisses her cheek as she smiles widely at him. The rest of the meal goes smoothly, and I decline their invitation to stay the night, opting for the long drive back to Paxton's house instead. All that time in the car has me contemplating decent date options with Toni and talking to Mike about a job. I'm not sure if working at the same place as my brother is a good idea. What if Mike sees my resume and decides I'm not good Sunset Security material. That would make it weird. It's time to talk to my dad. He's always been the one I go to if I need to talk things through. He understands me better than most people and has a pretty open view of the world. I'm sure he'll give me something to think about that no one else has.

THE NEXT MORNING, I roll out of bed early enough to run with Pax. I'm dragging a little because of my late return home last night, but it will be worth it to get some time with my brother.

"Late night? I thought you were staying in Miami."

"Nah, I wanted to get back here. It's crazy down in Miami. I did have dinner with Dev and Lucianna though."

"Yeah, I heard. Dev called me after you left, wondering why I hadn't talked you into working at Sunset yet." His right eyebrow rises, waiting for my answer.

"Let's run, I know you have to get moving early today. I'll fill you in." As we jog along the dirt roads near his house, I explain my experience from yesterday just like I did to Dev and Lucianna. My brother lived in San Diego for several years when he wasn't deployed, so he understands why I didn't care for the traffic and overwhelming feel of the city.

"So, I'm only going to say this one more time. Don't give me any shit about it either. You need to talk to Mike Wade about a job with Sunset. You don't have to take it, but at least talk to him."

"I don't need to follow you around for scraps in life," I tell him, my temper flaring. I rarely ever have issues with anger, in fact, I'm a pretty mild guy, but tagging along after my brother is a raw, exposed nerve to me. I may have been considering talking to Mike about the job on the way home, but my brother bringing it up again takes me right back to teenage me. To the sad, insecure kid who needed Pax for comfort and security.

Pax stops dead in his tracks, causing me to halt too and plants his hands on his hips. My brother doesn't have much of a temper either, not really, but apparently, I triggered it. "What the hell are you talking about?"

Squaring my shoulders, I face him head on. We're both breathing heavy, covered in sweat, and staring at each other like it's time for a schoolyard fight. "You know exactly what I mean. Since the day we met I've been following you, been your shadow. Everyone knows it."

"Bullshit!" He takes a few steps closer and glares at me. My brother angry is frightening, but I refuse to back down, not on this. I've felt this way since we were teenagers, and he took me under his wing. I was determined to stop following him around. It's the reason I went into the Air Force instead of the Navy.

"It's not bullshit. I followed you everywhere in high school. And when I went into the military, I know everyone assumed it was to be like you. Here I am, home from the military and whose house am I at? Yours," I shout, frustrated he doesn't get it.

Pax's eyes narrow, and his jaw flexes. "First, let's get this straight. You didn't follow me anywhere. I took you. I took you because I cared. You matter to me, you always have. You could even build a house on my property, and I wouldn't give a shit. In fact, I'd love it. I want you here. You're one of my best friends, one of the people I trust most in this world."

He takes a step back, and I remain silent, waiting for him to say everything he needs to. It's obvious he's not done; he's just formulating his next words. I've seen him do this over the years with our parents and my brother, Ben. "Your military career is the polar opposite of mine, but one you should be proud of, and it has nothing to do with me." He throws his hands in the air in frustration. "Okay, I took you a few places when we were in high school, so what? That's what brothers do. Ben and Renaldo did it for me. You earned your own grades, eventually your own friends, and you earned your own career accolades. This is what brothers do. They take care of each other. Call the others, and they'll tell you the same thing. I was in Ben's shadow for years. Then I earned my own place. You have too, you just don't realize it yet."

My brother's words hit the mark like an arrow on the bullseye and of course I feel like shit. He's right. He's never treated me like a burden or like his shadow. I'm not even sure where I got that idea. Probably because he spent so much time showing me around when I first moved in with them. It's just always stuck with me.

"And one more thing," he continues before I can say anything, "Mike Wade wouldn't hire anyone who won't help his business. He'd find a polite way of telling you that you're not the right fit. He's working hard to build his business and wouldn't jeopardize it to bring someone in who isn't qualified. If I didn't think you'd be an asset, I wouldn't have said a word and honestly I'm just a little bit selfish. I want you in Citrus County. I want my kids to grow up with Uncle Ferris around for holidays and sporting events and dance recitals. That shit matters and so do you. Now quit being a little bitch and call Mike when we get home."

He doesn't wait for me to say anything, he just resumes running, leaving me staring after him. I can't remember the last time he yelled at me, or if he ever has. After a few seconds, I shake my head and take off after him while his words roll around in my head like a snowball downhill.

When I reach the house and push through the front door, Shay pauses folding her laundry at the dining room table to check on me. "You okay?"

"Yeah, I'm fine. Is he?" I ask as I wander toward the kitchen to grab a glass of water.

"Well, he literally growled when I asked where you were before he stomped off to the shower. Did y'all have a fight?"

"Sort of. I was being stupid, and he called me on it." I take a long gulp as she watches me.

"I didn't know you guys fight. I know he and Chris sometimes argue a little, but never you."

"This is a first. I can't even remember us arguing when we shared a room in high school. I said something about following him around and being in his shadow and he kind of blew up."

"You in his shadow?" She laughs and goes back to folding as she talks. "How can you follow him? You were in the Air Force while he was in the Navy. Sometimes not even on the same continent. Maybe in high school, but I haven't ever heard anyone say that. I thought you had your own friends and clubs and stuff."

"I did." She's also making a point.

"He wants me to apply for a job at Sunset."

"I think that's a great idea. They need some brains behind all that brawn."

"You don't think it's weird to work with my brother?"

"People do it all the time. Mike's brother Thomas works there. It's not like you'll be providing the same function anyway. You complement each other well when you're together, I'm sure it'll be even better at work. Quit overthinking and apply." Shay grins at me. "I can say that because I'm famous for overthinking. I get it, but really, what's the worst that can happen? Mike and Hudson can say no, or you can work for them for some time and realize it's not for you. Or you can get a job you love, doing something you like with a great group of guys. And bonus, you'll get to see me a couple days a week since I'm still working there part time."

"Thanks, Shay." I flash her a little smile so she knows I'll be okay, and I head off to take a shower. I'll straighten things out with my brother later. I have a date tonight, and I need to figure out what we are going to do.

10

TONI

This date has me all wound up. In my head, I tick off all the reasons why my anxiety is through the roof. First, I have no business going out on a date. Between Ferris's uncertain plans, the situation with my dad, and the fact that the last guy I dated I then married, and he turned my father's company into a drug distribution hub, and we lost everything. Which says it all. Maybe I should call and cancel this fiasco before it becomes another crazy story in my life. My nervous hands smooth my shirt down, and I take one last look in the mirror before I go to the living room to wait for Ferris.

Gigi is already here, and she and my dad are watching old westerns on television. A young Donald Sutherland's voice is booming down the hall. Poor Gigi. When I reach the living room, both sets of eyes turn to me. My dad's soften instantly. "My beautiful baby girl. Where're you going all dressed up?"

I look down at my outfit. I'm not dressed up. I'm wearing khaki shorts, a nice blouse, and some cute sandals from my old life. I guess he means because of the makeup and jewelry.

"I'm going to dinner with a friend, Daddy. I won't be too late."

Gigi stands up and approaches me with the sweetest smile. She grips my arms. "You're too beautiful to be home early. We're fine. I'm ordering takeout tonight, and we have a John Wayne marathon starting in less than an hour. Enjoy yourself. Be young and have fun with the young man."

This is what I wish my mother was like, not the selfish, hateful woman I had. Tears prick the back of my eyes, and she must see I'm hanging on by a thread. She releases my arms and embraces me tight. It takes me a minute before I hug her back, but when I finally do, it feels so damn nice. So many times over the last couple of years I've needed a hug like this, but none were to be found. That makes me enjoy this one that much more. I allow a few tears to roll down my cheeks before I pull away and wipe under my eyes, hoping my mascara isn't smudged. Gigi grins at me and turns away as a knock sounds at the door.

One more swipe under my eyes, and I head to the door. When I pull the door open, Ferris is standing on the other side, wearing a turquoise and white checkered, short sleeve, button up shirt that's the perfect amount of dressed up without going overboard, a pair of gray shorts and slip-on boat shoes. With a freshly shaven face and the clean lines of a new haircut, I can tell he's already put more effort into this date than any I've been on before. His hand comes out from behind his back, and he hands me the saddest looking flowers I've ever seen in my life. I can't help but giggle. I was starting to think this guy is too perfect. "I'm so sorry. I planned to drop by the florist on my way here, but they closed earlier than I expected, and this was all the drug store had available. I wasn't coming empty-handed, but I considered throwing them out the window a few times because they looked so bad." His explanation and sheepish expression send me into a fit of laughter that has me doubled over. Little petals fall off one of the deadest of the bunch and I laugh harder. I can't even look up at his face to assess if he's mad that I can't stop laughing at his pathetic flowers.

It takes a minute until I get it under control, so I stand up straight and wipe under my eyes as he watches me warily, the first look of insecurity showing since I met him. I take two steps to get closer to him and rise to my tip toes and reach with my free hand around his neck to pull his mouth down to mine. I must shock the hell out of him because it takes a moment for him to respond. His arms snake around my waist, and he pulls me closer, smashing the poor flowers between us. The kiss is longer than it should be while we're in my doorway, hotter than the Florida summer night, and sweeter than the ice cream I hope to get for dessert. This guy can kiss, like world class, melt your panties right off, best kiss ever kind of kiss.

Finally, I release his neck and look up at him. "I'm sorry I laughed. That was the sweetest gesture, and those poor flowers look like I've felt for a long time. It just struck me as funny. Come in so I can put these in water." He follows me inside. Gigi is sitting on the couch beaming up at Ferris, as is my dad from the chair.

"Hello." I hear Ferris greet my dad who doesn't respond right away, which means he doesn't remember him. Ferris breaks the silence. "My name is Ferris Pearsall." My heart melts inside my chest like chocolate in the heat because he understood and did the nice thing, the perfect thing of rein-troducing himself instead of making my dad feel bad for not remembering him. I grab a tall cup and fill it with water. I didn't bring any vases with me when we moved because I never thought I'd get flowers again for any reason much less from a man. I set the cup with the sad flowers on the counter and smile at them. I love these more than a fresh, full bouquet, probably because they're truly all about the thought of doing something nice for me.

When I return, Ferris is sitting at the opposite end of the couch from Gigi who is still smiling at him while he talks about old westerns with my dad. I pause for a minute to enjoy watching the two men interact. This little bit of "man" conversation is so good for my dad, and the fact that Ferris is humoring him has my smile growing wider by the second. He's perfect. I should be looking closer at this, wondering why he's being so perfect, figure out what he's hiding, but I can't bring myself to do anything but enjoy the moment.

Twenty minutes later, we are pulling up to an outdoor seating restaurant on the Homosassa River. Thatched roofs and a live band give the feel of a tropical vacation destination. I've heard of the place but have never been here. Once we're seated, a twenty-something dark-haired server named Sammi takes our drink order and hurries away. A boat full of people pulls up to the dock to our left and everyone disembarks, moving straight to the bar—laughing and talking. A few kids run by on bare feet, headed for the little playground behind us. It's hot tonight, and humid even by Florida standards, but I'm still enjoying the atmosphere.

"Have you ever been here?" he asks as he closes his menu.

"No, people at the Lobster Lounge always talk about it, but I haven't had the time to check it out. I should bring my dad. As much as he loves the outdoors, he will really enjoy this. Have you been?"

"No, Shay and Pax came to this restaurant right before I came to stay with them and have been talking about it ever since."

Sammi returns to drop off our drinks and take our food order. Once she's gone, I finally ask what I've wanted to since I saw him last. "Tell me about life with your birth family. Do you remember them?"

He clears his throat and looks out toward the water. I wonder if maybe I shouldn't have brought up the subject. "They were great. My mom and dad were like everyone wishes their parents were, involved but not hovering, fun but not obnoxious. My sister was cool too even though she annoyed me half the time. There's not a day that goes by that I don't wish she was bugging me now. Although my adopted sister Courtney filled those shoes the best she could. My mom was a PTA mom, my dad taught the old people Sunday School class at our church. He liked a cold can of beer after cutting the grass, and she loved a couple of glasses of wine on a Friday night after work."

"I'm sorry I didn't mean to bring up something so depressing."

He glances down at his hand which is fiddling with the napkin around his silverware and back at me. "It's okay. I talk about them from time to time, I don't ever want to forget them. I just miss them. Everyone always told me that would fade, and they would just be a nice memory, but that's not true. It's as real now as it once was, I just have another family to help me get through it. That makes coping better."

"Tell me about your adoptive family."

He stops fidgeting with his napkin. "My dad, is tough but fair, and funny. I love the way he is with my mom, very much like my birth dad was except more publicly affection-ate. My mom, she's the glue for our family. Positive, loyal, strong, and compassionate, but she has a temper when she's mad, so she's not perfect. I just do my best to stay out of trouble.

"My oldest brother Benjamin is a prankster and a flirt, but also a devoted family man. Renaldo is next in line and is a bit of a troublemaker. Don't get me wrong, he's a good guy and has grown out of most of it, but if trouble were a treasure, he'd be rich because he used to find it often. My sister Courtney is married to a guy in the military, and they're stationed in Texas. She's the only biological child of our mom and dad, and she is just like my mom with an even stronger protective streak. You've met Pax and his family. To me they're the perfect family. They've seen their hard times, but they just keep fighting through and growing together. I envy them."

We sit quietly for a minute and sip our drinks before he continues. "Chris is the youngest and toughest of the bunch. He came from a terribly abusive home and saw his biological dad kill his mom. It took him the longest to adjust to life at the Pearsal's, but he's gained the most from it. He now has his own wife and son whom he worships. The man busts his ass to make a living, working a lot of overtime, but when he's home he dotes on Lena and Alex. I love to watch him with them, especially after seeing what he was like when he first came to our family."

"Okay, so tell me about your friends. You haven't mentioned them. Do you have friends?"

A deep chuckle comes from his gut. "Yeah, I've got friends. We're kind of the nerd squad. If you look any of them up in our old high school yearbook you'll see band t-shirts, bad haircuts, glasses, and complete goof balls. My friend, Jeremy teaches some kind of advanced physics classes at University of Florida. Marshall builds computers from scratch and sells them. He's the strangest of all of us since he's the conspiracy theory nut. I wouldn't be surprised if his windows and doors are lined with aluminum foil to keep the government from listening or some crazy shit. After another swig of his beer, he grins.

"Tyler is the most like me, though he didn't go into the military, he did go to work for the government and lives in Washington DC. He was married for two years before she left him for a lawyer. He hasn't really dated much since then. Great guy, a little intense at times, but he understands me better than all of them. Those are my high school friends. I have a couple of friends from my time in the Air Force who I will probably stay in contact with, but we will see.

"My friend Chance is driving here next week with his wife Aubrey, to bring me my motorcycle. I met them when I was on leave riding my bike through California after my last break up. I got ran off the road by some idiot driver and he pulled off the side of the road to help me. We just hit it off and we've been great friends ever since. They're a cool couple. Their pet isn't a cat or a dog. It's Esmeralda, the fainting goat."

That strikes me as so funny that I almost spit my drink out. He has to be kidding. "A what? A pet goat? Do they live on a farm?"

"Nope, it's a long story, but they thought they hit the poor thing with Aubrey's car and killed it when they were traveling. Turns out they didn't, this species of goat faints when it gets scared so when the car almost hit it, it passed out. They took it in and Aubrey fell in love with the thing. Chance acts like he doesn't like her, he calls her Mutton, but in truth he loves that damn goat. It's kind of funny."

"Mutton? What kind of name is that?"

"I don't know. He's Australian, so some of his words and terms are different."

"Will they bring the goat when they come out to visit?"

"No, she wouldn't fit on my motorcycle, and I think they have a goat sitter who is used to her fainting, so she'll stay with Esmerelda while they take the trip out."

"Why do they have your motorcycle if they live in California and you lived in Wyoming?"

"I was going to sell it to him before last winter since the weather is so crappy in Wyoming and I couldn't ride for so many months. Paying for storage seemed stupid and I didn't want to have to worry about moving it, so he insisted I just leave it with him until I got out of the Air Force. He said if I still wanted to sell it at that point, he would buy it from me. I think he knew I didn't really want to get rid of it."

"Sounds like a good guy."

"Yeah, he really is. I don't have a ton of friends, but the ones I have are true to the core. Tell me about you," he asks as he leans back and relaxes further in his chair.

"I don't have any friends left, except of course, the girls at work. Stacey has been really cool, since her ex was a complete tool too, so she gets it. The rest I lost over the years after being isolated while married to Lenny. Now, I don't have time to make friends. When I'm not working, I'm with my dad."

"That's a tough life for a young woman to live."

"Nah. I don't see it that way. Sure, some days I wish it were easier. I wish my ex didn't turn my dad's business into a place to traffic drugs, so that we could either sell it or pay someone to run it. That way it would still be bringing in money. Otherwise, I like spending time with my dad, even if sometimes he thinks I'm my mom."

"You're a good daughter. He loves you more than you can imagine."

We're quiet for a couple of minutes as we sip our drinks and listen to the music. The laughter of the children on the playground can still be heard behind us, and occasionally a slight breeze pushes through helping to lessen the heat of the evening. The rest of dinner is pleasant with Ferris telling me about life in Wyoming and stories about Lincoln and Morgan. I'm mostly quiet as I listen, finding the deep timber of his voice comforting and alluring at the same time.

Once dinner is over, he pays and leads me back to the car. His big hand engulfs my smaller one as we ride back to my place. I want to do something else, spend more time with him, something, but I also don't want to take advantage of Gigi. She's already at my house five days a week. Adding a sixth might burn her out, and I have no one else to help me. When we pull in the driveway my heart sinks a little. I don't want the night to end.

Before the date I worried about getting involved with someone who doesn't know where he'll be next month, or what he'll be doing. I worried about a lot of things, but right now all I can think about is the fact that I don't want him to leave. I want more time holding hands, I want his kisses and want to be surrounded by that calm relaxed aura he has about him. Being with him settles my soul, which should scare the shit out of me, but tonight it doesn't. Tonight, it's worth the heartbreak that will likely happen in a few weeks when he leaves.

He shifts in his seat so he's facing me and tucks some of my hair behind my ear and takes my chin between his thumb and pointer finger so gently. "What's on your mind? I can tell that you have a squirrel running circles in your head."

His blue eyes burn into mine. God, he has no idea his appeal, the allure he has for a girl like me. "I was thinking how I wished I didn't live with my dad so that you could come in and stay longer. I'm not ready for our date to end."

"But..."

"But like I told you earlier, I don't want to take advantage of Gigi. She's—"

His thumb covers my lip, cutting me off. "You don't have to explain. I also don't have to leave." He leans in closer, so close I can feel his breath. I lick my lips, my heart pounds so loud I swear he can hear it. His eyes close and his mouth meets mine. Our lips part and our tongues meet, slowly at first, doing the teasing dance of a beginner's kiss, but quickly heating up and turning into more. Before I know it, one of his hands is in my hair controlling the direction of the kiss while the other one slips under my blouse and rests on my bare skin. There was a sexy little sizzle under my skin when we pulled into the driveway just from a great night out and his hand holding mine, but with the intensity of the kiss and his hand under my shirt I practically burst into flames.

Reaching down, I put my hand over his and guide him higher until it's over my bra and on my breast, showing him what I want. His fingers trace the edge of the lace bra I'm wearing and my body quivers in response. I nip his bottom lip and reach a hand under his shirt. Smooth skin over tight muscle. God, it feels so nice. When he shifts a little, both of us trying to work around the console, and dips his fingers into the cup of my bra, pulling it down and tucking it under my breast, I shiver. His kiss grows hungrier, and I moan as he pinches my nipple lightly. When he switches to the other breast, following the same pattern, I hiss. "Ferris"

He removes his glasses and sets them on the dash board. With his lips he trails across my cheek and down my neck, stopping to nip the skin just slightly near the base until he reaches the swell of my breasts. When he pauses and his warm breath skates across my hardened nipples I shift restlessly. If ever there was a time I needed relief between my legs, it's now.

"God you're gorgeous," he groans before suckling on one nipple while toying with the other. I swear I'm about to orgasm just from the feel of him at my breasts. That's never happened. In fact, I'm not sure I've ever been this turned on, especially in the front seat of a car.

He suddenly pulls away, and I'm left feeling cold as the air conditioner blows over my exposed chest. I can't process the abrupt change until he hits the button on the side of his seat to move it backward. "Climb over here, honey. I need you closer."

I want to shout hell yeah and leap across the seat. Instead, I unbuckle my seat belt and scramble across the seat in the most awkward and unlady-like way possible. Me climbing over the console to share a seat is not as easy as it was when I was a teenager. Soon I straddle his hips, and we're face-to-face with nothing in the way except the steering wheel against my back. I feel him between my legs in the sweetest way. I rock my hips slightly and let my head fall back pushing my breasts forward. He lifts his hips and groans so deeply I can feel the vibration across every inch of my skin. One of his hands snakes around my back and holds me still while the other grips my breast so he can feast from it. It's like I'm being worshiped, which is something I'm not used to from a lover. I can't control my hips as they rock against him. The feeling of him between my legs, hard, huge, and hot is heaven. Curiosity is killing me though. I want to see what his shorts are barely concealing, but there isn't enough room to work that out. I do my best to push the thought of seeing him naked out of my head and enjoy what he's giving me right now, but my imagination, coupled with the pressure against my core has an orgasm barreling through me in seconds. I cry out my whole body shaking in his arms. His lips switch to the other breast, and I shudder harder, unable to handle the goodness that's overtaken me. Finally, I fall forward and rest my forehead against his shoulder.

Ferris is rock hard between my legs. I'm sure he's hurting for relief, but I'm so far gone I can't move to try and alleviate the situation. He taps my arm, and I sit up. Gently he tugs my bra cups back into place and adjusts my shirt.

"I have to move you on back into your seat so I can get this situation under control. Then I'm going to go inside with you, and we will finish the night watching the John Wayne marathon with your dad."

"You can't go in there like that. I can't leave you that way," I reply, almost horrified at the thought of him walking into our house with a hard-on and knowing there is no way to hide it. Also, knowing he will be miserable as he watches John Wayne save the world from bad guys.

"If you give me a couple of minutes to think of something unattractive, I might be able to settle things down. I'm not going in there like this, and you aren't taking care of it." He glances down at the bulge in his shorts.

"What if I want to?" I inquire as my hand grazes the bulge in his shorts.

He removes my hand and laces our fingers together. "To be blunt, the first time your hand or your mouth is wrapped around me is not going to be across the console of a vehicle in front of your house. But I have to be honest right now, you can't be touching me, and we have to change the subject because neither is helping me get it under control."

I can't help but glance down and giggle. "You're probably right. So how 'bout them Rays?" I ask switching the subject to baseball, even though I know nothing about it. His body shakes with his chuckle, and all is right in my world for just a few minutes.

11

FERRIS

Holy Shit! I assumed she'd be beautiful all over but seeing her shirtless was way better than my imagination. The thought of her completely naked has my cock throbbing in my pants like a first timer at a strip club. I was able to settle down and go inside with her and say goodbye to Gigi. We started watching television with her dad who fell asleep in his chair a little bit ago. Things were okay until she rested her hand on my thigh. Now that's all I can think about. It's ridiculous.

"Let's get your dad to bed," I prompt her, knowing I need to either leave or get her dad out of the room. I'm not going to make out with his baby girl while he's in the same room no matter what illness he suffers from. That's not cool.

Fifteen minutes later, he's resting in bed. During the time it took her to get him ready for bed I had plenty of time to think and realize I need to leave. It's not the gentlemanly thing to do to stick around to make out more.

"I'm going to head out," I tell her.

"Why?" Her shoulders sag and the wrinkle in her forehead gives away her confusion.

"I don't want—" I start to explain but she ignores me, grabs my hand, and pulls me to the couch. Then she changes the channel on the television to a music only station and yanks me down on top of her. I probably should have left; this is not what I wanted to happen. Okay, maybe I did, but that was the irrational part, not the part that wants to treat her with respect. The problem is my mind veered the other direction tonight in the car out front and hasn't been on a logical path since, no matter how hard I tried.

We both ignite the minute our lips meet. The chemistry between us is like nothing I've ever experienced. Her legs wrap around my hips, and her fingers score my back as I grind against her. I'm either going to come in my pants or leave here with the worst case of blue balls I've had since I was seventeen years old and had my first date. Just as we're readjusting so I can get my hands under her shirt, a loud pounding on the door jars us both. Surprised, I leap up from the couch, my breath heavy. "You expecting anyone?"

As she's shaking her head, the pounding starts again and is accompanied by yelling. "Toni, open the door! I'll break the damn thing down!" a man shouts and I know that voice.

"Shit! What's he doing here?" she shrieks and leaps up, adjusting her clothes and heading for the front door.

I grab her by the arm harder than I intend. "Don't open the door to someone who's this hostile," I growl.

"That's my ex. If we don't open it, he'll break it down or wake the whole damn neighborhood, especially my dad." She shakes free of my hand and stomps toward the door, so I hustle over behind her. She's not opening that door without me at her back. He needs to know she's not alone.

"Lenny, what're you doing here? What do you want?" she yells at him as she opens the door to three men. The one in front is Lenny and he's moving closer to her as he talks. The other two are standing back quietly, with stern expressions like sentries.

"Gimme the keys to the warehouse. I need them now and I'm done fucking around. You don't seem to understand the severity of my request. I've left you several messages, you know this." He's talking though clenched teeth and all I can think about is knocking them all out. I can't believe this asshole has been calling her.

"Oh, I understand, but I can't help you. The DEA took all of that from me when they seized the property. Why do you think I ignored those messages? I can't help you, nor do I want to. You need to leave before I call the cops!" her voice has risen with each word until she's practically shouting at him.

He doesn't even flinch at her response before he reaches for her neck, he's quick and she doesn't have time to evade the maneuver. That's when I lose it. I pull her back and come down with a hammer fist hard and fast on his arm, causing him to release her and fall forward. It only takes me a second to have him out of the doorway and face down in the yard with his wrists behind his back and my knee digging into his kidney.

One of the guys lunges for us, and I do a quick leg sweep he doesn't expect and knock him flat on his back. I release Lenny and nail the other guy in the throat with a hammer fist. Quickly, I switch my attention to the third guy who is already moving toward me. Springing from the ground, I rush him and nail him right in the gut with my lowered shoulder and flip him on to the ground. Lenny was slow to roll over during all this, but he's back on his feet ready to face me again. I'm calm as I wait for him. I know he'll lose patience before I will. It doesn't take him long to move in close enough to take a swing, and when he does I catch his fist and use it to spin him so I can wrap my arm around his neck. He struggles, but I have the leverage, and by the time it's all said and done I have him in a choke hold, cutting off his airway. His hands claw at my arm as his panic sets in.

"It's time for you to go. Toni told you she didn't have the keys. If you come back, I'll have you arrested for stalking and assault after I kick your ass. You got it?" I bark at him as I tighten my hold on his neck momentarily before letting up enough to for him respond. He tugs at my arm unsuccessfully. "Yeah, man, fuck you. I got it. If she would just—"

I squeeze again. "No, she's not required to do anything. She's not gonna to do anything for you ever. You need to back off."

About that time, the dragging and clinking sounds of a walker break the silence that follows my directive. I turn my head slightly to see that her dad has joined us and is standing at the door in his pajamas. Toni is half way between me and the doorway.

"What's going on?" he wonders aloud as he takes in the scene before him.

Toni rushes over to him in a feeble attempt to block him from getting a good look at what's going on. "Oh, Dad, you shouldn't be out of bed. Everything's okay."

He shrugs her hand off his shoulder and glares at her. "It's not okay when banging and yelling wake me up. It's the middle of the night."

"I see the old man is still looney as hell." The asshole in my grip mumbles. I squeeze him harder, causing him to squirm again.

"Shut up. It's time for you to go, and I swear to God, if you come back, I'll do more than embarrass you."

I yank up one more time just to cause more pain and make my point. I release him with a little shove to his back.

Lenny stumbles slightly before he rights himself, glances down and starts dusting off as he's moving away from me toward his vehicle, mumbling bullshit the whole way. How did she put up with this guy for so long?

Paul looks at Toni. "What did he want?"

"He wants a key to the warehouse, but I don't have it. You don't have it. He needs to leave us alone."

"I should have known something was going on. I ruined our whole lives."

"Dad, I told you before. It's not your fault. He was sneaky, and you're sick. There is no way you could've known. It's okay now. He's gone, and you can go back to bed. Don't worry another minute about it."

His sad eyes shift to me and back to his daughter before he nods and shuffles back inside, the clicking of the walker and shuffling of his feet the only sound.

"Go help him. I'll shut the doors, and then I want to look at your throat before I go home."

About twenty minutes later her dad is settled again and she comes back out. "I'm sorry such a great night got ruined."

I hold out my hand to her, and she grabs it. With a gentle tug I pull her between my legs on the couch and place my hands on the back side of her thighs to hold her in place. "Tonight was a great night. I'm pissed your ex keeps bugging you, but I can't say it didn't feel good to put him out of commission. I call that a win for the night. Let me see your throat." She tilts her head back, and I examine the slightly reddened area. "I don't think it will bruise, but it pisses me off he got his hands on you. When I leave, I want you to lock up behind me. If he comes back, call 911 immediately. Don't open the door and don't reply to him."

I push her back a little and stand. Then I take her mouth

in a kiss I hope she goes to sleep thinking about and stride to the door. "Come lock up. I have an interview in Tampa tomorrow, but I'll check in with you at some point. If you need me, call me and I'll be here."

WHEN I PULL out of the parking lot in downtown Tampa, I feel good about the interview. I liked the company, the person who interviewed me, and even the building where I would work. The downside is Tampa traffic. It's not a huge city, but there is enough traffic to put it on the con side of the pros and cons list. So far though, this is my best prospect. It's the perfect fit for me and my skills. When I leave, I jump on highway 275 and head over to Thomas and Simone's house, who are waiting for me.

We are halfway through dinner when Thomas finally brings up what everyone else keeps mentioning. "Why don't you apply at Sunset Security?"

I shrug, trying to decide how to answer that. He leans forward, and I wonder if my brother has called ahead to prompt him. "I'm telling you, you won't regret it. It's a great job. Always something different going on. And even though Mike's my brother, he's still a great boss."

"You're starting to sound like, Dev, Pax, and Shay."

"It's because we're smart. You have skills that would help us, and we need good people on our team. Tell him, Simone."

I switch my focus to her to see her hands held up in front of her. "Oh no. Don't bring me into this. Maybe he doesn't want to work with his brother and your brother. I'm not telling him to take a job that might make him miserable." She forks another bite of grouper into her mouth and chews, her eyes shifting between the two of us.

"It's not that. I respect your brother, and I'd probably like working for him. It's my brother who's the issue. Not because we won't get along or whatever. It's more because I don't want to be his shadow. I don't want to follow him around everywhere like when we were teenagers. I don't know. It's complicated I guess."

Thomas rests his fork on his plate and sits back, his eyes studying my face for several seconds. "I get that better than anyone. Growing up as Mike's younger brother, you have no idea how big a shadow he's always cast for me to live in." He shakes his head and chuckles. "But what I do know is that you and your skill set will be valued, the flexibility is unmatched, and the pay isn't bad either. Besides, I think your brother will love it. You guys are as close as Mike and I are. I know my brother, and he's serious about his business. If he doesn't want you for what you can bring to the table, he won't hire you. Your brother would be a good reference, it would get you the interview, but Mike won't hire someone just because they're related. In fact, he would probably think harder about it. Just think about it, especially if you want to stay in Crystal River. From what you're telling me, it sounds like you might."

My mind keeps replaying his words as I finish my dinner. Thank goodness Simone changes the subject to Gavin—her son from a previous marriage who is with his father this week. When I finally make it back to Citrus County, it's past eight in the evening. And although I'm tired, I want to check on Toni. It seems irrational to be thinking about her as much as I have been, especially since I need to be concentrating on my future, not a woman, but I can't seem to help it.

The parking lot is packed at the Lobster Lounge so I park in the next lot over and walk to the front door. The weather is warm and muggy, which makes sense since I heard we have rain coming some time tonight. The noise level alone as I enter tells me the place is at full capacity. There's a family of five milling around by the hostess stand waiting to be seated. Dishes and glasses clink and the usual murmur of conversation throughout the building is up several decibels where you can't hear the music blaring from the speakers in the ceiling.

The servers are hustling between tables filling drinks and delivering food. It takes me a moment to spot Toni, but I finally do when she rushes out from the kitchen with a tray filled with food on her shoulder. Although her hair is pulled back, little wisps of stray hairs have come loose and are floating around her face. Cheeks flushed and eyes intent, it's obvious she's been busting her butt this whole shift. I decide not to bug her, so I stroll over to the bar and take the one lone barstool at the end. Nick greets me with a warm smile. "Hey, man. How's it going?"

"Good. Looks like y'all are slammed. Has it been this way all night?"

"Oddly enough, it's been this way all day. I think every local and tourist in town decided the Lobster Lounge was the go-to place tonight. Not that I'm complaining. Tips have been great. I'm sure the ladies will say the same, there hasn't even been time to take a quick break."

"Damn, man. I'll make it easy. I want a Red Right Return. I already ate so I'll just sit here and watch the game over your head."

"Works for me. It's so bad I haven't had a chance to check the score. He turns around and glances at the television. "Rays beating the Orioles, sweet. I'll catch the replay tomorrow. It's my day off, and I don't plan to do anything but lay on my couch and catch up on television. My wife might have a different idea, but after I show her my tips she'll agree I earned a veg on the couch day."

Once the glass is full, he slides it over to me with a smile. "You gonna be here 'till closing?" He glances up like he's looking at Toni across the room, indicating he knows why I'm there.

"Yeah, I'll be here. Take care of your customers. I'll be fine." He lifts his chin and moves to the other end to fill drink orders for one of the servers.

Two and a half hours later, the place is finally empty. The servers have been cleaning as they go, and now Toni is perched next to me on the empty seat rolling silverware. "I swear, if I could invent anything, it would be a machine that rolls the damn silverware. It's the last thing I want to do at the end of the night. I don't mind the rest of the side work, but this. Ugh. It's tedious and feels like it's never ending."

I chuckle. "Why don't you let me roll and you finish the rest of your work."

She looks horrified at the suggestion. "I can't let you do my job."

"Sure you can. I'm not doing anything, and if we tackle this together, we can get you out of here faster."

She must really be tired because she only hesitates for a second before asking, "Are you sure? I feel like a jerk letting you help me."

"Of course, I'm sure. It benefits me too, you know, to get you out of here sooner." I wink at her playfully.

She grins. "Okay, slave away. You have to finish that whole tray."

"No problem."

Within thirty minutes we have everything done, and

she's standing in front of me with her apron off, purse over her shoulder, and a happy grin on her face. I slide off the stool and take her hand, leading her out to the parking lot.

"Can we take a walk or something? I'm not ready to go home yet. I just want some fresh air, even if it's humid enough to melt us both. Being inside all night, especially when it's busy, is suffocating."

"Sure, any thoughts on where you want to go?"

"A customer told me about the dock near Hunter Springs Park. Let's check that out. It's right around the corner."

"All right, jump in with me and I'll bring you back to your car afterwards." When we pull up to the park, it's pitch black with no soul in sight. "Are you sure you want to walk around here? It's pretty dark."

"Are you afraid of the dark? I'll protect you." Her sweet flirtatious voice has me fighting my dick getting hard.

"I'll hold you to that. Stay where you are. I'll grab my flashlight and get your door for you."

"You don't—" she starts, but I hold up my hand to cut her off. "Don't. Both of my mothers taught me manners, and that includes opening a door for a lady. Let me do my thing." She nods, and her lips tilt up as if she likes what she's hearing from me.

We walk the short distance across the gravel parking lot to where the boardwalk starts and further toward the water. A few of the houses across the water still have their lights on. My eyes adjust to the darkness, and hers must too because when we reach the railing she asks, "Can you kill the flashlight?"

"Yeah."

She releases my hand and leans her elbows on the railing. It's quiet minus the crickets and the frogs. A deep bellow a little further away is inconsistent but present too. "What the heck is that?" she asks.

I press my front to her back and rest my hands next to her elbows and whisper in her ear. "A big ole gator. They make that deep sound. I swear it's their mating call. Looking for some late-night action, but my dad says it's just a sound they make."

"Your dad knows a lot about gators?"

"My dad knows a lot about a lot of things, but especially Florida wildlife. He grew up here and has spent years hunting, fishing, hiking, and enjoying it all. When we were young, he would take us out on the boat or to his friend's hunting camp. The whole time he would school us on the wildlife, the trees, the water, everything, as we hunted or fished with him. He said we couldn't really appreciate it if we weren't educated on it. As annoying as it was when I was young, I get it now, and I'm thankful."

"The most outdoorsy thing I did was horseback riding. I loved riding, the wind in my hair, the sun on my face. Not to mention the horses themselves. I miss them the most. But other than some birds, bugs, and snakes I didn't encounter too much. A rat ran out in front of me in the barn once, and I lost it." I chuckle against the skin of her neck as I lean in close. "Well, we can remedy that. What would you like to try outdoors first?"

"You know what I'd really like to do?" Her voice rises and octave as she continues excitedly before I can guess. "I want to go on one of those manatee tours where you snorkel around with them and just watch them in the water. It seems relaxing and kind of freeing, the way I feel when I ride horses, but in cool water." She smiles wistfully. A few of my customers are the private captains who run those tours and they talk about it all the time. I've thought about booking one and ask if my dad can come out with us and sit while I swim. He would love that. I'm just not sure how you would get a man in a walker on a boat."

She shrugs and grows quiet. I'm going to figure out how to get her and her dad on one of those tours. I can't help but want to do things for her. Anything that will make her smile.

After a minute or two, she turns in my arms and our faces are millimeters apart. "I can't tell you how nice it was to see you at the bar watching the game. I knew you were there to see me, and that felt so good." She places her hand on my face, slides it around to the back of my neck and pulls until my mouth meets hers. If this is her way of showing gratitude, I'll break my neck to give her more to be thankful for.

The kiss grows more heated as they always seem to with us, and her hands shift to move up under my shirt so her nails can dig into my skin. I groan and press myself against her to show her what she's doing to me and slip my hand under her T-shirt. Her skin is damp from sweat and hot against my fingers. She moans, and my hand drifts down into the band of her cotton skirt and over the cheek of her ass to pull her tighter against me. She hikes her leg and changes the direction of the kiss to grind against me. Little drops of warm rain hit the back of my neck and arms. "It's starting to rain," I warn her.

"Don't care. I forgot to mention this is something else I'd like to do outdoors," she murmurs as she trails her lips down my neck. It feels so good, chills run down my arm that have nothing to do with being cold. Before I know it, she's fumbling with the snap and zipper on my shorts, and her hand is reaching in and releasing my rock-hard cock. My head falls back, and I groan.

Her hand slides up and down my hard flesh as she licks

and lightly sucks along my neck. The rain falls harder and runs down my face. I push my glasses up on my head and reach down to hook her knee with my hand, opening her up to me and guide her leg around my back. Thank God, she's limber. My fingers press in and run across the damp fabric between her legs. Toni's breath hitches, and I know she's ready. I wrap my fingers around her panties and yank. She gasps, and I'm sure she'll have a fabric burn from that maneuver, but she obviously doesn't care because she pleads, "Please, Ferris. Please."

God, can I have sex with her right out here in public? I want to so bad, but that wouldn't be right. What if someone comes out here? The rain falls harder, soaking us both. My flashlight gets knocked to the deck and rolls away.

She grips me harder. "Please Ferris, don't make me beg more. I need it." I open my eyes to find her shirt plastered to her breasts, her nipples perky and perfect. I pinch one lightly, and she growls, pulling me down to her again going at my mouth like a starving woman, and I lose all control.

The rain is making this slippery and even more sexy. "Wallet. Condom." Is all I say, and she's pausing to dig in my back pocket. She fumbles with my wallet and drops it to the deck once she has what she wants. She lowers to her knees and before I know it my dick is in her mouth. Oh, my God. I didn't expect it, and damn does it feel amazing. She takes several pulls, making my eyes roll back in my head, and my breath catch. She finally rolls the condom on and stands back up, her eyes meeting mine. The desire, the need, the hunger. I see it all in her eyes and it removes the lingering worry about taking her right here and now on this board-walk deck in the rain. Rivers of water run down her face and neck, over her chest as it heaves with her heavy breaths. I squat to grip her behind her thighs and lift her up. She falls forward into me and wraps her arms around my neck and her legs around my hips. I press her back against the railing and push inside her warm channel. Her head falls back, and she calls out my name. I pause and let her adjust to our position and my depth. "Damn, you feel so good," I mumble into her neck.

"Yes, yes, move, Ferris, come on." I cannot get enough of the begging. I hope this is a constant thing with her.

"As you wish." I groan as I thrust, starting slowly, building it for both of us. Our mouths connect in a sloppy, sexy, emotional kiss, and my hips buck harder. Her nails dig into my neck, and her sex clamps around me and spasms in the most mind-bending way, pulling my orgasm out of me. She leans forward and bites my neck as hers rolls through her.

Holy shit. That's the most insane sex I've ever had, and that's saying something considering I dated a stripper with a wild side.

"Dear God, that was unreal." She breathes against me, and her body shivers against mine.

"Are you cold? You have to be. We're soaked," I ask as reality sets in that I just took her in the most ungentlemanly fashion, in a public place. Of course it's late, dark and rainy, but still. I should have had more control, more respect.

"That's not exactly how I would describe what I have going on," she jokes, and I can hear the smile in her voice. I sigh relieved that she's not sounding regretful.

"Come on, let's get out of the rain." Carefully, I lower her feet to the ground. Her sigh is heavy as she adjusts her clothes and grabs her torn panties off the dock. I tie up the condom and shove it in my pocket before I put myself back together. It takes a minute to find the flashlight and turn it back on. Then we head to the parking lot hand in hand.

Once we get back to the car, I find the little cloth to clean my glasses and dry them off. She has her contacts in tonight so doesn't need it.

Then I return her to her own car, wishing I could continue the night with her in my bed. However, with her dad under her roof, and me living with my brother, that won't happen. I need to get my life in order, and either back away from Toni or find my own place.

12

TONI

I t's been three days since the sex on the dock. I've thought about almost nothing else since that night. It was a little embarrassing walking into the house to face Gigi soaked and disheveled. But she didn't ask any questions, and I didn't offer an explanation. Ferris and I talked on the phone once and texted every day since, but his friend Chance came to town from California, and he's been busy doing the tourist thing. I wish my life was normal enough that he could invite me along to join him, and I could meet his friends and have a few drinks in the middle of the afternoon with them at one of the riverside bars in the county. But Gigi is the only one I trust to stay with my dad, also the only person I can afford, and she needs time off too, not to mention I wasn't invited. I'm not sure what to make of that. I can't decide if he's just saving me from having to say no, or if it's that he doesn't want me to meet his friend, or if this is just so temporary he's not bothering. I really hate this in-between spot we've put ourselves in. I'm afraid to ask what we are to each other and prematurely end the beautiful time we have together by trying to put a label on it. But

I am a woman, slightly insecure at times, and now that we've made this intimate, I can't help but feel a little more attached.

Today has been another long one at work. We had a full house tonight which made my shift fly by and my tips amazing, but I'm tired. Nick walks me to my car and waves as I pull away. When I reach our condo, I turn off the car and sit there for a second, thinking about how different my life would be if I wasn't taking care of my father. If my ex-husband hadn't smuggled drugs through our family business, and if my mother hadn't left with her latest piece of ass. How I came from that woman is still a mystery to me. She has zero care for anyone other than herself. I sigh and head inside.

Entering the house, I notice that it's oddly quiet and the hair on the back of my neck raises. Even when my dad is asleep, I can still hear sounds from the television and Gigi calling out to me as soon as I open the door. That's not the case tonight. As I step into the living room, my blood runs cold. Gigi is face down on the floor, blood pooling around her. The room is destroyed. *Oh my God!* Dropping to my knees, I pull her over onto her back and check for a pulse. My fingers fumble on her wrist and don't find anything. I move up to her throat. Sweat forms on my brow as I move my fingers looking for the right spot. I can't find it, and my panic grows. *What if she's dead? Holy shit! Not Gigi. Oh God.* I finally find the right spot and locate a light pulse against my fingertips.

"Argggg," she groans, and I cry out in relief. Stuff drops out of my purse as I fumble to dig my phone out and dial 911. I quickly explain what I walked into before the realization hits. The television is smashed in the corner and the contents of all the drawers are thrown all over the floor. It looks like a tornado went through the room.

The 911 operator explains that they are sending an ambulance and as she's saying something else I become aware of that fact that I don't see my father. "Dad," I whisper in realization. I was so shocked to find Gigi faced down it didn't register he's not in here. I drop the phone and yell, "Dad," again as I rush out of the room, praying he's okay and not laying in blood in his room or the bathroom. As I run down the hall, I find more shit everywhere. My room looks even worse than the kitchen. My dad's room is empty, but in the same state. The bathroom is torn apart, even the toilet tank cover is shattered across the bathroom floor and all of my tampons are strewn everywhere. I race back to my phone and hang up the 911 call. The only person I can think of is Ferris. He'll know what to do. I hit go and after two rings Ferris picks up with a smile in his voice. "Hey beautiful, I'm out right now. Can I call you when we get home?"

"No. No! My dad is gone. Gigi's hurt, badly. The ambulance is on its way. I need your brother. I need to find my dad. Please, help me." I yell into the phone, my whole body tense and shaking.

"What the fuck?" he snaps, his sweet demeanor switching to anger in an instant. "Stay calm. I'll call Pax and Mike. I'm sure the police will arrive with the ambulance. Tell them what you know. I'm on my way. You can tell me everything when I get there. Hang tight, baby."

"I'm scared," I confess, my mind whirling with horrible possibilities and my body trembling.

"I know," he tells me before I hear him bark a few orders at whomever he's with and come back to me on the line. "I'm on my way. Stay with Gigi, make sure your door is unlocked for the paramedics."

"Okay, Okay. I'm..." I stall, suddenly at a loss for words.

"It's okay. Just stay calm. I'll be there soon. I'm hanging up to call Pax."

The line goes dead, and I return to Gigi. Where could my dad be, and why is my house a wreck? What could someone want from a waitress and her elderly father? When I kneel down next to Gigi and press a kitchen towel I found on the floor by the stove to the wound on her head, she winces and opens her eyes. She squints trying to focus on me. "I'm sorry your dad...." She trails off and tears start to slide down the side of her face.

"Who was it?" I lean in and ask urgently, hoping she will answer before she passes out again.

"Lenny," she croaks.

"Son of a Bitch," I yell, causing her to cringe away from me. I soften my tone. "I'm sorry, Gigi. Do you know where they took him?"

"No," she croaks.

It's then that the paramedics enter through the open front door. "Over here," I call out to them.

They're in the middle of their assessment when Mike Wade comes through the door, his eyes cataloging everything in the room before he says a word. There is a police officer right on his heels. Mike reaches out and pulls me into his arms to hug me tight. After a few long comforting seconds, he asks quietly, "You okay?" He pulls back and looks down at me.

"Yes, no. I don't know. Gigi will probably be okay, but they think she has a concussion. I don't know where my dad is, but it was my ex-husband who took him. I don't know where they went. I don't even know where he lives anymore. I don't know what to do."

"Don't worry, we'll find him. Talk to the police while I call Pax and Hudson. Where is Ferris?"

"He's on his way. He was out with friends." I barely get that out when Ferris jogs through the door his face flush, forehead wrinkled with concern and eyes wild. He pulls me into his arms like Mike did. "Are you okay?" He holds me closer as he waits for my answer, and I snuggle in tighter, liking his arms around me, needing them. I nod against his chest.

"Tell me what happened." He lets go and leads me to the chair my dad usually sits in and crouches in front of me.

"I worked, and then I came home. When I got here, Gigi was on the floor bleeding and unconscious. My dad was gone, and the house looked like this." I wave my hand out, directing his attention around the house.

The policeman standing behind him interrupts. "Sir, I need to ask her some questions."

Ferris stands and moves to my side. "Of course. I'm just going to listen."

"Mrs. Gonzalez said it was your ex-husband and his associates who did this. Do you have any idea why?"

"He came here looking for a key to our old warehouse last week, but Ferris sent him on his way. I told him we don't have it. The government seized all the property and probably changed the locks. Either way, I don't have them. My dad can barely remember his name, he doesn't have anything hidden anywhere either. Why Lenny thinks I can get him in there, or even want to, is beyond me. My dad though. He has dementia, and his health isn't good. My ex has a horrible temper, and there is no telling what will set him off." Fear and guilt clench my heart, and I realize I was just in the car wondering about being normal. I'd rather be abnormal and take care of my dad than have him taken from my life too soon. I rub my hands over my face.

"I'll be right back. I need to go tell Mike what I know. What's your ex's full name?" Ferris inquires.

"Leonardo DiSalvio."

He strides out the door, and I finish answering the officer's questions. The lead paramedic turns to me. "We're taking Mrs. Gonzalez to the hospital. Can you notify her family? She needs stitches, and she has a concussion. I'm sure they'll want to keep her for observation."

I step over and grab on to her hand. "I'm so sorry, Gigi. I'll call your son, and I'll be there as soon as everyone gets out of my house."

"Don't worry about me. Find your dad. My son will come take care of me. I'm sorry I couldn't keep them out."

Tears run slowly down my face even as I fight showing emotion. "It's not your fault. I'm sorry I didn't realize he was a threat. I'm sorry I left you here like a sitting duck."

"It's okay, sweetie. Give me my phone and my purse. Call my son, and I will call you tomorrow." She gives me a shaky smile meant to make me feel better, but it only makes me feel worse.

Two hours later I'm in Pax's truck in the passenger seat as Aubrey, the wife of Ferris's friend Chance, drives me back to Pax's house. What a horrible way to meet Chance and Aubrey, in the middle of a kidnapping. Everyone decided it was a bad idea for me to stay at my place. The guys loaded up and are headed to the old warehouse. I'm not sure what the police involvement is, but they documented everything at the house and said they were handling the kidnapping. I'm trying not to think about it, but I'm freaked. My ex has obviously lost his mind, and I'm certain he'll hurt my father if he hasn't already. That doesn't even touch the fear I'm feeling for all those men heading out to hunt him down. As crazy as my ex is there is no telling what he will do. Ferris promised me they would find him or turn Florida upside down looking, but now I'm concerned that one of them will get hurt helping me.

"Don't worry. It's going to be okay. Ferris told us all about Mike and Pax and what they do at Sunset Security. They're more than capable. Chance did a stint in prison, and I know Ferris can take care of himself."

"I just hate that they're putting themselves in danger. I knew my ex was an asshole, but I didn't realize how dangerous he was. I don't think Ferris kicking his ass in front of me and his buddies helped the situation, but he deserved it. I'm just worried, and don't get me started about my dad. His mind is already fragile, his body is not much better."

"I get it. Let's just get back to Pax and Shay's house. We can grab a beer and relax while we wait, or you can go crawl into Ferris's bed and get some sleep. I'll wake you up when we hear something. You must be exhausted."

"I can't sleep. A beer sounds better. I hope we don't wake anyone up at their house."

"We'll be quiet. Shay knows we're coming. Pax didn't want us to freak her out, but he didn't want us to go back to my hotel. I think they felt better knowing we were safe out on their property."

Once we arrive at Pax's house, Shay meets us at the door in a robe and hugs me tight. "Don't worry, they'll get him back."

"I'm so sorry we're messing with your sleep. I know the kids will have you up early."

"Don't worry about it. I work in the office at Sunset. I know what jobs they normally do. Mike and Pax know what they're doing. They'll bring him back. With Ferris and Chance helping it's going to be fine."

"Thanks for everything."

"You want to go lay down in Ferris's bed and get some rest?"

"Nah. I just want to sit and try to calm down. It's been a long day, but with all this going on there's no way I can sleep."

"The porch swing hanging out front is the place I'm able to find the most peace when things are crazy. I know it will be harder with this situation, but it may be worth a try. Let me get you something to drink. Are you hungry?"

"No, thanks, but I could use a beer."

"Make that two if you don't mind, Shay. I'll hang with Toni. You go back to bed."

Shay reaches in the fridge and pulls out two bottles of beer, pops the tops, and hands them to us. "Make yourself at home. Come get me if you hear anything. My room is right back there." She points to the hallway. "If the kids didn't get up so early I wouldn't desert you two."

"Seriously, don't worry about us. We're going to wait for the men on your porch swing," Aubrey explains. Shay nods once and quietly returns to her room. We grab our drinks and make our way to the swing. The night is quiet except for the crickets singing in brush surrounding the house.

"Take my mind off things. How did you meet Chance? Did you take a trip Down Under and drag him back with you?"

She chuckles. "You would never believe it. I met him at a rest stop when I was moving from Wisconsin to California. It's a long story, but we ended up on a road trip. Then he ditched me in Vegas after we got married."

"You met and married him on that trip?" My eyes grow huge. That seems crazy.

"It was a fake wedding performed by a fake Elvis. Long story, but basically, he was going to prison for attacking a man who hurt his sister and didn't want to tell me, so he slipped away during the night. I mean I probably wouldn't have told me either. I was super uptight at the time and an attorney, but it wasn't good."

"Feels like I'm missing something since he's here with you." I wait because seriously, if I wanted something to take my mind off my life, I hit the jackpot.

"When he got out of jail, he came looking for me. I was engaged to someone else, and he just kept showing up until I couldn't ignore him anymore. Hell, to be honest, the moment he showed up I went into a tailspin."

"Do you two have any kids?"

"No, just Esmerelda Snowflake."

"Ferris told me about your pet goat."

She grins at me and takes a swig of her beer. "I know it sounds crazy to have a goat as a pet, but if you met her you would understand. She's just so sweet."

"I'll take your word for it." We swing quietly for some time. Although it's nice and would be relaxing under other circumstances, I'm too antsy to sit for long so I stand up, stretch, and check my phone. I'm not a patient person in the first place, add my elderly dad being kidnapped by my crazy, drug running ex-husband and my nerves are shot, and the miniscule amount of patience I had is gone. I begin to pace back and forth in front of the swing as Aubrey watches me. She doesn't comment. I'm hoping she understands, but if not, I can't care too much right now.

After probably a half an hour, she must have grown tired of watching me pace. "Do you enjoy being a server?" she quietly inquires. She doesn't sound judgmental, just curious.

"Yes, it keeps me busy and gets me out of the house. Sometimes people can be rude or impatient, but overall, I enjoy it. I probably wouldn't choose it for a lifelong career, but for now it pays the bills so I can take care of my dad."

"If you could choose any job, anywhere, what would you choose to do?"

I stop and stare at her. I've never been asked that, but I know the answer. I think about it every day. "I'd take care of horses. My dream would be to have a piece of land with a little house on it and a barn." I don't elaborate on it more. "Maybe someday."

I turn to look at the darkened dirt road that stretches in front of the house as the dream plays out in my head. Four or five horses with their faces sticking out of their stalls looking to me as I enter the barn. The soft hair as I brush them, the sound of their hooves pounding the ground as I ride them around the property, and the soft chuffs of happiness as I feed them carrots. Hell, even mucking the stalls doesn't sound so bad. Those big, beautiful beasts are calming for me. They always have been. All my free time was spent in our horse barn growing up. My mom was crazy and demanding, not in a good way, and my dad worked a lot. With no brothers or sisters there wasn't anyone to entertain me. That left me with the horses. I miss them and the peace they brought to my soul.

A few more minutes go by before my nerves get the best of me again. "I can't stand this wait," I mutter as I begin to pace the length of the porch once more. Aubrey watches me silently. Her face doesn't show it, but I'm sure she thinks I'm nuts. My ex-husband is angry and crazy. That's a terrible combination when your elderly father with dementia is in his care. Especially when Lenny hates my dad. It takes the patience of Job on a good day. I can't imagine how it's going, and all the things my brain can conjure up are not things I care to think too hard about. "I'm sorry. I can't sit still. My dad is all I have. I've built my whole life around keeping him safe and happy, and now I can't do either. It's out of my hands, and I want to claw Lenny's eyes out."

"I get it. I wish there was more I could do." Before she can say more, her phone buzzes with a message. After she flips it over to read it, she exhales loudly. "Hopefully it will be over soon. They found them. Chance is staying back. Ferris, Mike, and Paxton have just gone in the warehouse after your dad. They know where they're holed up and are going to try to flush them out. The cops have the building surrounded. Just say a little prayer that no one gets hurt."

I drop in the rocking chair and rest my elbows on my knees as I breathe deep trying to keep calm. My muscles are jittery, and my mind is running through every nasty scenario there is. What if something happens to my dad? What if something happens to one of the guys? Oh God. I breathe deeper. The fear is driving my anxiety higher.

Aubrey's hand rests gently on my back. "In through your nose. Slowly. Out through your mouth," she commands quietly. I listen to her words as she repeats them a little louder this time. Focusing on her voice, I follow her instructions. In and out. In and out.

"It's going to be okay," she reminds me. I continue to breathe slow and deep as silent prayers of hope run through my mind. Although this is so much sooner than I expected to hear from anyone, the fact that we don't have any information on how my dad is actually doing, only an idea of the scenario that could get any number of people hurt or killed is almost too much for me to deal with. Time drags on so slowly. This waiting game is almost physically painful. It seems to last forever but is probably only forty-five minutes to an hour.

Finally, Chance calls back, and I watch Aubrey's expressions carefully, but she shutters her reaction making it hard for me to tell what she's feeling. Once she hangs up with only a few words on her end, she relays the information. "They're taking your dad to a hospital in Ocala. Mike is riding along to get a couple of stitches because he got a flesh wound from a bullet graze. They asked me to take you to the hospital to meet your dad. When Ferris is done with the police, he'll meet you there. I can ride home with the others at that point. Everyone is okay. Your dad's in rough shape, but he's alive."

She's pulling me into a hug as she delivers the information. My body and mind are suspended. Halfway between thankfulness that we know what's going on and fear that my dad's trip to the hospital is for things I may not be able to handle.

"Aubrey, oh, God." A strangled sigh comes from somewhere deep down and my muscles turn to jelly. The tears begin to flow and my shoulders shake. Aubrey lets me go on for a few minutes.

"It's going to be okay. Come on, pull yourself together. You can do this. I know you can." She holds me tight for a minute, and I focus on the hug, stuffing it all down. She's right. Now is not the time. I need to take care of my dad; I need to be strong for him. I straighten my spine, swipe at my tears, and swallow hard.

"Come on. Pull yourself together. Let's tell Shay what's going on. She can lock up as we leave. I know you'll want to be at the hospital to talk to the doctor. Besides they'll need you for paperwork." She grips my shoulders tight for another couple of seconds before she turns and goes inside to get Shay. Within a minute, she's back, and we're padding down the front steps on our way to the hospital.

Aubrey plugs in the address to the hospital and pulls down the dirt road. I stare out the window, praying to God that my dad is okay and that all this drama isn't too much for Ferris. I realize he's moving away from here, but I would hate for him to associate negative feelings with me. Because I know my heart will always smile when I think of him. Somewhere in this short period of time I've come to care for him more than I should. Maybe it's because of the way he is with my dad, or maybe it's because he's so sweet with me. It could also be because he risked his own life to find my dad for me. It doesn't matter why. All I can say though is that whatever it is, I feel something for him, something more than I've felt in a long time.

BY DAYBREAK, my dad has been admitted for observation. With several broken ribs, multiple bruises all over his body, and a concussion, not to mention my dad's overall health, the ER doctor decided it was best to monitor him. I think he was also taking into account that I would have a hard time caring for him in our current situation. Ferris joined me an hour ago, and Aubrey left with the guys.

My dad dozes off, and Ferris sits in the chair next to my dad's bed in the ER. He pulls me into his lap and settles me in against his chest. We were told we would probably be waiting a little longer to get him into a room. I'm exhausted and emotionally wrung out. So much so I haven't even asked what happened to Lenny. Truthfully, I don't care unless there's a possibility he'll come back for us. I'm hoping he'll get locked up for good this time. No getting out on bond.

As much as I would like to slip off into dreamland like my dad, I can't seem to shut my brain off. "We don't have a car here," I whisper.

"It's fine. Once we get your dad settled in a room, I'll get us a ride home. Don't worry about it. Let me take care of you, okay?"

"I'm sure you have other things to do today besides deal with more of my crap."

"Nope. I'm good. Got the whole day free. I know you're used to handling everything on your own but let me do it today."

I'm too tired to fight, so I nod against his chest and relax. "I need to call my boss. I'm supposed to work tonight. There's no way I can do it though."

"They'll understand. You can call in a couple of hours when they open."

"You're right. I just keep thinking, and thinking, and thinking. Every time I close my eyes, something else runs through my head."

He wraps his arms around me a little tighter and kisses the top of my head. "I swear it will be okay." The feeling of his warmth surrounding me, and the strong steady tone of his voice, reinforce his words, and I try to shut off my mind. I slip into a light sleep for a brief time until the nurse finally comes in to let us know they are moving my dad to a room upstairs.

"They'll need some time to get him settled. I think it's best if you come back later this afternoon after you get some sleep. Your cell phone number is in the system, if anything changes, they will call you"

"But, what if—"

She places her hand on my arm to stop me. Her expression is sweet and understanding. "Don't worry. He's in good hands. You won't be any good to him if you're wiped out. Go get some sleep. You can come back later and see him when you're rested. It's what's best for everyone." I don't argue, I just stand as a nurse's aide and an orderly come in. "You head on out. He'll see you later."

I stand, lean over, and kiss his forehead. "I love you, Dad," I whisper and then allow Ferris to lead me out of the ER and into the parking lot where he stops at a Toyota sedan and opens the rear passenger door. "This is my parents' car. Climb in." I'm so tired and wrung out emotionally I want to cry, instead I slide into the car and plaster a smile on my face the best I can. This is not how I wanted to meet his parents. His father turns slightly and shares a sweet grin. "Hey there. I'm Ray Pearsall, and this is my wife, Audrey. We've heard a lot about you. I'm sorry about your dad."

Ferris climbs in the car on the other side and slides over to wrap his arm around my shoulders. The gesture is so comforting I want to melt into him and sleep for a week. Instead, I do my best to remain polite. "Thank you. He's going to be okay, or as okay as a man with advancing dementia can be. It's been a long night. I appreciate you picking us up. I'm sorry to put you out."

"Nonsense, honey," Audrey's soft voice says from the front seat. "It's no problem at all. We could use a few hours in Crystal River to see our grandkids anyway. It's a good excuse."

I remain quiet on the ride to my house as the gravity of the night presses down on me. Any little bit of energy I had is long gone, but the weight of the world is on my shoulders in full force. Ferris talks quietly with his parents about his job interviews, and I block them out because, honestly, I can't think about him getting a job and moving away. I know we haven't been seeing each other long. I know I have no right to wish he'll stick around Crystal River, but I can't stop my heart from hoping and my mind from daydreaming.

When we turn into my driveway, I see Ferris's truck and my car side by side, and I get a little warm inside. It's totally lame to make the his and hers connection in relation to us. It's not like its toothbrushes next to each other on the counter—something infinitely more intimate.

Nope. It's just two vehicles side by side.

I open the door and climb out quietly before leaning back in. "I would love to invite you in for something to drink, but honestly I have no idea what my house looks like after last night. Will you take a raincheck?"

Audrey's eyes smile tenderly at me. "Oh course, sweetie, you need to get some rest anyway. Maybe Ray and I can come take you guys to dinner one night."

"I would enjoy that. Thank you again." Ferris wraps his arm around my shoulders and pulls me back a few steps so that they can pull away. They're both grinning and waving as they go.

"I have no right to ask this, but I'm worn out and emotional. I could really use your arms around me as I sleep. Will you stay?"

His lips brush my forehead as he pulls me tighter against him. "Of course. There's nowhere else I'd rather be." He leads me inside, down the hall, and straight to my bedroom ignoring the mess around the house. We push the mess off the bed and onto the floor to join the rest, knowing I will have to clean it up later and I curl up in his arms and drift off.

13

FERRIS

All the reservations I had about asking Mike Wade for an interview with Sunset Security are gone. During the rescue mission for Toni's dad, I realized my skills could be useful for his team, and we worked well together. It didn't matter that Pax and I were brothers. The only thing that mattered was executing the mission as safely as possible and utilizing everyone's skill sets in the most productive way possible. If I had time to plan, I could have been a bigger asset in helping safely conduct that mission.

The longer I think about it, the less I understand why I was being such a tool about approaching Mike for a job. Sometimes the insecurities from my youth reach up like a hand around my throat, closing off all rational thought like air. It's crazy and irrational but so deeply ingrained it's hard to break free of once it starts. I hate the circumstances that helped me realize I was being stupid but am appreciative of the peace and understanding it brought to me on more than just my career path. It also illuminated the fact that I would move mountains if necessary to make sure Toni Armstrong is taken care of and happy. My desire to make sure she doesn't have to worry about anything anymore is so strong.

I texted Chance and Aubrey to let them know we were going to get some sleep before we meet up. I feel bad they drove my motorcycle all the way out here, planning to spend time with me, and instead got stuck in the middle of a crisis and are now entertaining themselves. Thank God for them being here though. Aubrey ended up being a comfort to Toni and helped keep her sane. As for Chance, let's just say his skills with his fists came in handy, even if only briefly. I'm so appreciative for good friends.

We slept soundly facing each other with her head on my arm and one arm thrown across my waist. My arm is numb and tingly because of our position, but there is no way I'm moving it with as comfortable as she is. Her hair is all over the place. Some across her cheek, nose, and mouth, and the rest all over the pillow like she came out of a windstorm. With my index finger, I shift the hair away from her nose and mouth as gently as possible, but she stirs. My body was awake and aware of her before my brain was. I should be embarrassed I can't get it under control, but I can't help the way I react when she's near. Her eyes flutter open and crinkle with a morning smile.

"Morning, beautiful."

"You're awake early," she observes.

"I'm lying next to a beautiful woman. My body knows better than I do that I shouldn't waste the moment."

"Sweet talk in the morning will get you everywhere." She snuggles in closer and places a kiss on my pec. "I should probably brush my teeth, but I don't really want to move and break the magic spell."

I chuckle. "Magic spell?

"Yeah, a handsome prince is practically naked in my bed. No one is being kidnapped, no evil villains are in my front yard, and no forgetful fathers are asking me to cook breakfast."

I'm thinking Toni might be the woman for me. She can make light of recent events, no matter how traumatic, and smile the next morning. "Handsome, huh?"

"Yeah, even without those sexy as hell glasses," she quips.

"My glasses have never been referred to as sexy," I tell her.

"Some guys have naughty librarian fantasies, I have my own version of that, but more like a Clark Kent kind of way. Superman is way sexier than some librarian named Mona wearing pencil skirts and button up blouses." When she finishes her statement, she places a few more kisses on my chest and grazes my nipple with her teeth. That sends a zip of energy to my groin.

She doesn't expect it when I shift us quickly and efficiently to brace my arms on both sides of her and rest my hips between her legs. Her alabaster skin looks like porcelain in the morning light—fragile and smooth. "God, you're beautiful."

A shy smile tips her lips. I don't give her time to say anything else, I dip my head and kiss her lips once before I work my way lazily across her jaw and down her neck. She squirms when I hit the magic spot and lifts her hips to press us tighter together. I grind against her just to hear her softly moan my name. "Shirt off," I whisper against her skin. Wiggling and squirming beneath me, she manages to tug it off and toss it to the floor. Her perky breasts are bare, her nipples straining for attention. I work my way across the soft mounds, kissing and licking, avoiding the sensitive tips until she's shaking and begging with need. When I finally suck her nipple into my mouth, she arches up and threads her fingers into my hair, holding me to her.

"Ferris, more."

I pull with my lips and flick it with my tongue before switching to the other breast. Her fingernails dig into my scalp fueling me on further, working for the same reaction. Finally, I work my way down across the soft skin of her belly and bury my face between her legs. Her curls tickle my nose as I swirl and dip my tongue along her most sensitive flesh.

"Ferris," she cries out wriggling and grinding against my mouth. When she pulls my hair, I know she's close. I slip two fingers inside her tight channel and pump them in and out over and over as my mouth works harder. It doesn't take long before her body pulls tight like a bow and her cries grow louder, until finally, her sex grips my fingers, pulsing with her orgasm, and she falls limp against the sheets. I slide back up her body and kiss her, willing her to taste herself on my lips. She wraps a leg around my hips and rubs against me, already ready for more.

My cock was hard before, but now it's throbbing. Her fingers slide down my torso and into my boxer briefs. With one hand on my ass and the other over my shaft I'm about to lose it. I flip over and take her with me, so she's perched above me.

"Grab my wallet on the nightstand. There's a condom inside." She grabs it, tears the foil, and gently rolls it down my length. I grip her hips and help shift her so she can slide down. Her body is even tighter after her orgasm, and I clench my teeth, willing myself to calm down so it's not over before it even starts. My hands roam her skin until she begins to move, slowly at first, rising and falling her eyes never breaking contact with mine. It doesn't take long for her to build a mind-blowing orgasm in both of us. Toni changes the motion of her hips, her breasts bounce, and my hips buck up to meet hers. The sounds of flesh smacking and heavy breathing fill her room, fueling me on. I grip her hips tighter.

"Fingers between your legs, I can't hold back much longer." The sight of her pleasuring herself as she rides me sends me spiraling over the edge. I continue to push up into her until she finds it again and collapses on my chest.

It's official, with the chemistry we have, and her resilience and heart, I'm not letting her go. I hope she's ready for me because I'm not going anywhere.

SEVERAL HOURS LATER, I've been to my brother's house, showered, shaved, and changed clothes. I'm slightly human again and ready to go back to Toni. I swing by the hotel and pick Chance and Aubrey up. They're sporting matching sunburns across their noses, and I'm betting in a few other places too, but they look relaxed and happy. "This is a bit of paradise here, mate."

"Y'all must have swum to Three Sisters Springs today?"

Aubrey answers excitedly before Chance can. "Yes. Summer and Mike took us on a river tour and parked outside the spring. We swam up the little canal into the spring, and it was breathtaking. It looked like something out of a movie. I was shocked. And can you believe that a movie star spent the day with us? Just swimming in the river and sunning on the boat with us? How cool it that?"

"Summer's cool that way. Very un-Hollywood."

By the time we pull into Toni's driveway, she's standing out front watching us with a small smile. Her hands are clasped in front of her and she's rubbing her thumbs over each other. I noticed her doing that the night I met her at the Lobster Lounge when she kind of insulted me without meaning too. Why is she nervous? After the way things have progressed with our lives, and the things we've experienced in the last twenty-four hours, she has no reason to be nervous with me or my friends. In fact, she should be more comfortable knowing people care and have her back.

I step out of the car with a warm smile in hopes it releases any tension she might feel. Almost instantly, her shoulders relax and lower, and she flashes me a bright grin. I place a soft kiss on her mouth and usher her to the car, opening the door so she can sit in the back next to Aubrey.

"How's your dad?" Aubrey asks.

"Resting comfortably. I feel bad I didn't stay long, but the nurse said he's been sleeping most of the day and is calm when he's not, so they suggested I use this time to relax and take a break. I'll go early tomorrow. We still aren't sure how the concussion will affect his already sketchy memory, so it's a good idea for me to take a break now while I can."

A quick glance at her through the rearview mirror confirms she's okay even if I can hear the sadness in her voice. "You guys look a little pink. What did you do while we slept the day away? I'm sorry for that by the way. I know you're here to see Ferris."

Chance is the first to reassure her, and it's not the first time in the last couple days I'm thankful for such a great friend. "No worries. We had a great day. Swam in the springs, saw a dolphin, an otter family, and a couple of manatees. It was cool. Next time we know to add more sunscreen, hence the pink noses. The hardest part was keeping Aubrey from trying to steal an otter to take home. It's bad enough we have Mutton waiting for us." He chuckles, and I can see Aubrey glaring at him from the backseat.

"Do not call Esmerelda Snowflake Mutton. It hurts her feelings."

At that we all burst out laughing. "I still can't believe you named the goat Esmerelda Snowflake," Toni chokes out as she laughs.

"She's unique. She needed a name that reflected that," Aubrey says with a bit of defensiveness to her tone. We laugh more, and when I glance back, I find Aubrey fighting a smile. I'm sure it has something to do with the fact that she's able to make us laugh after what we experienced just last night.

"Any word on what's going on with Lenny?" Aubrey asks.

"He's being held without bond. They're planning to bring multiple charges against him. Apparently, he was looking for cocaine and fentanyl that he had stashed in the ceiling tiles above my dad's office. Not sure how the DEA missed that in their original search of the building, but they did. Lenny recovered it and had it on him when he was arrested this time. The guys he was supposed to be moving the drugs for were going to kill him if he didn't get that stuff to them by tomorrow night. Not sure what he's going to do now. I can't imagine he's safe in jail with the rest of the inmates. I've seen enough movies to know if a gang wants you dead they can make it happen while you're in custody. Honestly, I don't care though. I'm just glad he's not going to be running around free any time soon." Everyone nods in agreement, and they all let the subject drop.

We drive south and find a nice place to have dinner in a town called Tarpon Springs, home of the famed Greek sponge docks. It's a neat outdoor venue with a killer menu and live music. The meal is excellent, the conversation is better, and holding Toni's hand under the table through most of the evening is the best. Once dinner is over, we drive Chance and Aubrey the rest of the way to Tampa and drop them off at the airport hotel to catch the red-eye back to California.

Right after we drop them off, Toni's phone rings. "Who is it?"

"It says Citrus County Sheriff's Office."

"Well pick it up." I encourage as I nod toward her phone.

She talks in one to two words sentences for a couple of minutes and finally hangs up. "They caught the couple who slashed my tires. I can't believe it." She sighs.

"How? When?"

"Earlier today. A neighbor of theirs called the cops. She said they were at their house for a barbeque, got drunk, and were bragging about slashing my tires. They even went so far as to share a plan they had for the future about following me home and going after my dad. The neighbor was smart enough to tape them with her cell phone once she realized they were serious about what they planned to do to me. I guess they aren't well liked in the neighborhood, and their level of crazy freaked the neighbor out enough that they felt they had to do something about it."

"That's insane, but we knew they were stupid. I'm just glad they were that stupid and their neighbors were that smart." I grab her hand across the console and squeeze.

Once we're on the toll road headed home, we fall into more comfortable conversation, the deeper getting-to-know-you kind, and I find that I like everything about her. Even the weird little thing she does where she rubs her thumbs over each other when she's nervous about something.

"So tell me what your future looks like," I request. Her

thumbs start to stroke across each other again, and she looks out the window into the darkness. "Hey, nothing to be nervous about. We're just talking," I encourage as I grab her hand and lace our fingers together again.

"It's just that I've lived so long not looking to the future, I don't know what it looks like. I never know how things will be as my father's dementia progresses. With it being just me and Dad for the last few years, I never had anything to look past tomorrow for. Does that make sense?"

"It does, but I want you to think hard and tell me, in a perfect world with no obstacles, what would you want. Do you want to go back to school and get a degree? Do you want a family? What would make you happy and fulfilled." I'm asking because my heart is telling me to find a way to make it all happen for her. Find a way to help bring out her brightest smile every day. I can't do that if I don't know what her hopes are. It sounds stupid if I say it out loud, so I won't, but I'm going to do everything I can to help make her dreams come true, and I'm going to love every minute of it. She may not know I have a plan yet, but I do.

It only takes a few minutes to find out that she's never had any interest in college or trade school. She wants to spend her love and energy on horses. I let her words and thoughts that seem to come out of a vault pour between us for the next half an hour. Her excitement and happiness is infectious. I also find it interesting Aubrey asked her almost the same thing just last night. I need to remember to thank Aubrey for that, or I may not have gotten all the information I wanted in this short time. Their conversation got her thinking.

As we're pulling into the driveway, Toni's phone rings and a quick glance at the screen reveals it's Gigi calling. The tension jumps back into Toni's muscles almost instantly.

"Hello?" I help her out of the car as she carries on the conversation with her friend, and I can hear the sadness and fear in her voice as she asks questions and offers to take care of the medical bills. By the time the conversation is over, I'm still not able to decipher how things concluded with them.

Once we're through the entryway and the door is closed and locked behind us, I lead her to the couch and pull her down into my lap. The house is still a mess and we will have to clean things up, but not right now. I'm more concerned with Toni. "Tell me about it," I whisper against her hair.

"She isn't blaming us. Doesn't want me to pay her medical bills. She's being sweet about it, but she's not able to help with my dad for the next couple of weeks, so I have to figure something else out. It's possible he won't be able to come home for a few days, so that will help, but I'm not sure what to do when he does come home until her return. It's not like there's a back-up sitter, and I certainly can't afford to take off work until then." Her sigh is heavy, and I can almost feel the burden she's carrying. "Let's not talk about this tonight. After such a nice evening with good people, I don't want to ruin it with sad conversations. I want to pretend like I'm a normal woman, being held by a handsome man, alone in my house with no possibility that someone will walk in on us."

The mere suggestion has me growing hard beneath her. She leans back and kisses my jaw, and I close my eyes, savoring the feel of her lips against my skin. I slide my hands up the outside of her thighs and under her dress. Her skin is so smooth beneath my fingertips. I trail them back down until I reach her foot and push the cute little sparkly sandals to the floor. She cranes back almost awkwardly, searching for my mouth, so I grip her hips and lift, repositioning her so she's facing me and straddling my lap, her most precious parts pressed against mine.

Our lips meet slowly at first, and her fingers slide into my hair, her nails scraping my scalp gently. Sexy, hot, and sweet. My hands slip up the back of her dress to her bra strap. I unhook it and slide around under the fabric to graze the underside of her breast. So soft, so plump. Perfect. Her breathy little moan as she leans into my touch is almost my undoing. I fight to keep control as my thumbs rise higher to graze her hardened nipples. With each swipe of my thumbs, she rocks against me. And when I add my finger to pinch them, she pulls away from our kiss, her head falling back, her moan louder. A quick shift and shuffle, and I'm pulling her dress over her head and tossing it to the floor, followed immediately by her bra. She's perched on me like a goddess with all of her beautiful skin exposed, breasts high, nipples beaded, hair hanging down her back, and her eyes are full of lust and something else I can't quite place. I lower my head to draw her rosy nipples into my mouth scraping them gently with my teeth. Her hands grip my head and hold me to her as if she needs more.

Her desire fuels me, and I work her harder with my caresses, lips and teeth for each little mewl, groan, and hip roll she gives me. Wrapping my arms around her to hold her in place I stand and twist, so her legs are against the back of the couch.

"Turn around," I whisper to her as I tug on her ear lobe, drawing a shudder from her. I whip my shirt off, and it joins her dress on the floor.

With one hand, I work on the button and zipper to my shorts while the other traces its way around her abdomen and dips into her panties. When my fingers make contact with the damp heat between her legs, I shudder and yank my shorts and boxers down my legs one-handed. I don't want to take my fingers away from the little slice of heaven at the center of her. As I explore and find the perfect spot and rhythm, her hips move with my fingers in perfect harmony to get friction on her engorged clit. The motion of her bare ass against my dick has me weak in the knees. I pull my fingers free and bring them to my lips, needing a taste. Her neck cranes to watch what I'm about to do.

As the tangy flavor of her sex melts against my tongue she begs. "Ferris, please. I need you inside me. Don't make me wait."

Who am I to deny her what we're both dying for? I bend over and grab a condom out of my wallet. "Knees on the couch. Elbows on the back. Brace, baby. I don't know how gentle I can be right now."

I tear the foil packet open, roll the condom on, and lift my gaze to her perfectly round ass. I grip both of her hips, my hands wrapping almost all the way around and line myself up with her opening. I ease in as slowly as I can, not wanting to hurt her. She's still much smaller than me, no matter how wet and ready she is. With excruciating slowness, I push in until I'm completely seated inside her. Her heat, her grip, and the sight of her body poised in front of me to take what I'm going to give is almost too much. My balls pull up tight, and my cock swells. She feels so good, like I never knew possible. My body bends to conform to hers, and my hands snake around to grip her breast with one hand while the other slips down to caress her clit.

I hate that I can't see her expressions, but I love the control I have of her body like this. The urgent fear I'll come before we even really get started abates, and I flex my hips slowly, stroking in and out of her wet pussy. Her breathing is labored, the muscles of her sex clench and unclench as she pushes back against me, urging me on. We work together, driving us both higher. Sweat slides from my hair line down my brow line and over my neck. I'm practically melting I'm so hot for her right now. As my thrusts grow harder, her moans turn louder until she finally bucks back against me, clenches tight, and shudders her climax. I lean back, grip her hips even tighter, and begin a brutal rhythm until I practically explode within her and collapse against her back.

The sweat from our bodies is the only thing between us as we both catch our breaths. I pull out, tie off the condom, and drop it in the trash can in the kitchen. When I return, I find she hasn't moved, so I twist her and lift her into my arms. This time I carry her to her room with no plans to come out until the sun comes up.

LAST NIGHT WAS by far the best night of my life. The chemistry between us is off the charts, but the simple touches and caresses of her fingers are heaven for me. For a guy who has spent so much time alone, it's a bonus to have that constant tender physical touch. I'm not sure how I got so lucky to find her, but I plan to keep her.

My meeting with Mike Wade is at his office at 11:00 AM. Once I've showered, shaved, and printed a copy of my resume, I'll head over there. For the first time since I left the Air Force, I'm feeling like the future is bright. For so long it was just... uncertain. Now, I can see past the interviews to a house and a family, and time with Pax, Shay, and the kids, as well as my other siblings at barbeques and family gatherings. How it all changed in such a short time, I'm not exactly sure. Maybe it didn't. Maybe it started the night I met Toni, and I didn't realize it until I was knee-deep in some covert operation to get her dad back safe and sound. Or maybe it was when I was buried to the hilt between those pretty thighs. I don't know, and I don't really care. It's just nice to be looking at the world and life in general through rose-colored glasses for a change.

When I pull down Citrus Avenue to the Sunset Security offices, I notice several cars and trucks parked out front, and I have to park farther down than usual. I grab the folder holding my resume, straighten my tie, roll my shoulders, and move toward the door. The first person I see is Shay, sitting behind the desk with a big smile. Morgan spots me from across the room and beelines for me with her arms in the air squealing the whole way. I set my folder down to grab my niece and toss her into the air.

"Hey, Sweet Pea. How's my girl?" I ask as she grants me her four teeth smile.

"I was running late, so she had to come in with me while I did a few things. I'll drop her off at the sitter for a couple of hours once you guys go into the interview. She's a little hellion these days." Shay's tired chuckle tells me she loves it, but she's also worn out. I make a mental note to watch the kids one of these days so they can have some time to themselves. "Here, give me the slobberpuss, they're all waiting for you."

"They?" I ask. I thought it would be just me and Mike. A sliver of unease fractures my confidence a little.

"Hey. Don't worry. It's all good. Just head on back."

Morgan squeals in discontent as Shay pulls her out of my arms. I lean in and kiss both of their cheeks, grab my folder, and head back to the conference room. When I walk in, I note Mike at the head of the table, Hudson to his right, Pax to his left, Dev next to Pax, and Thomas across from Pax. What the hell is going on? They all stare at me, none of them giving anything away with their eyes. I had no idea Dev and Thomas were in town.

Mike speaks first. "Grab a seat down there, Ferris."

I pass him the folder and sit down. Mike leans over and yells toward the door. "Hey, Shay, can you make a copy of this for me please?"

When she comes through the door with a squirming Morgan in her arms, squealing for Dada we all chuckle, which helps me relax for a brief second.

"How many?" she asks.

"Five, keep one and scan it for our files, please."

"Sure, give me a second to wrestle a baby gator." She hustles out of the room, and I can hear her talk to Morgan as the copy machine churns out the papers. No one in the room says a word. I still can't figure out why everyone is here and in on my interview. Pax didn't mention they do group interviews or that he would be here this morning.

When Shay returns, she passes Pax the papers, kisses his cheek and tells everyone, "I need to drop her off at the sitter. I can't get anything done with this special helper. See you in a half an hour." Everyone says goodbye, and the resumes get passed to each member of the team.

They all quietly review it. I take off my glasses and wipe the lenses with my tie. It's a nervous gesture, but I need something to do while they look over my resume.

Everyone finishes reviewing my files at the same time except Dev who takes about thirty seconds longer.

Finally, Mike addresses me. "Honestly, it's totally unnecessary for us to be here. At least as far as I'm concerned." My heart drops to my stomach at his words. "You could have had the job the day you drove into town. After working with you the other night on our impromptu mission, I'm even more confident you'll be a good fit for the team. But I needed you to know that every member of this team has recommended you because of the man you are and the skills you'll bring to the table."

My heart races, and I'm sure my face flushes. That's not what I expected him to say. I'm not sure what it was, but this wasn't it.

"We all know you because of Pax, but that doesn't make you Sunset material. The computer and analytical skills you bring to the table, the black belt in jujitsu, and the quality of the man you are does. I wanted to make sure you knew without a shadow of a doubt that every man on this team wants you here."

Hudson, always the quiet man in the room, slides a folder I didn't even realize he had across the table to me. "Review that, it's your employment offer. It includes insurance, but the salary is nonnegotiable. If you perform like we think you will, we can discuss a raise in ninety days."

I open the folder and look down, excited about what's inside. Normally, I would wait until I'm back at Pax's in the privacy of my own room, but curiosity about the offer is killing me. The first thing that jumps out at me is about halfway down the page. The salary is double what I made in the Air Force and comparable to what I was being offered by Sonavive Tech in Miami.

When I glance back up, everyone is staring at me, waiting for some kind of response except my brother who is flat out smiling. He knows I won't pass this up.

I close the folder. "Let me review this tonight, and I'll get back to you tomorrow," I say with the straightest face I can muster. The cock-sure grin my brother is sporting falters, and I bust up laughing. "Awe, what the hell, I'll review it more closely later, but yeah I'll take the job."

The guys all clap and whoop like we're at a football

game or something, and I can't help but laugh. Who knew the nerdy kid with no family would someday be sitting in the room with some of the finest men he's ever known and be recruited to be part of their team? Not me, but I'm sure glad for the hand fate has handed me this time.

14

TONI

Dad got out of the hospital yesterday, and today is my first day back at work. Gigi is still healing, so Ferris offered to take care of Dad. To be honest, I'm a little nervous. Not because I don't think Ferris can take care of him. I'm more worried Ferris will see what a headache it can be to take care of someone full-time and go running for the hills. I haven't seen him much over the last few days since I've been at the hospital so much, and he's been busy with family stuff. I almost wonder if I've scared him away, or if he's just busy. The logical side of me says everything is fine, but the nervous, nothing-goes-my-way side of me has me feeling fidgety and insecure.

My phone dings from my pocket with a text message and I pause to pull it out thinking it's Farris. To my surprise it's Aubrey. "Hey lady! How's your dad?"

I grin. "Better than when you were here. Still healing though. Farris is watching him today."

"Good, you know he's in capable hands. Just wanted to check in on you."

I send her back a smiley face and a heart and shove my

phone back in my pocket. Who knew I would gain a friend from all that craziness that happened? I didn't expect it, but we have been texting and I'm appreciative of her.

Work flies by, and if I weren't so on edge about Ferris, I would enjoy the bustle of a busy night. Instead, I'm a little distracted and in a hurry for work to be over. The last table lingers forever, drinking long after they're done eating, and my side work takes forever so I don't get home until after midnight. Everything is quiet when I enter. There's no flicker of the television, only the glow of a lamp by the couch. My dad is nowhere to be seen, and Ferris is sitting on the couch with a book in his hand and his feet up on the coffee table. The soft smile on his face says he's relaxed and comfortable, and I'm hoping happy to see me.

He sets the book down on the coffee table and pats the spot beside him. "Come take a load off."

I move toward him, and he speaks again. "On second thought, sit down at the other end of the couch and give me your feet."

"What?"

"Just do it," he says with a mischievous grin.

Too tired to argue, I do as he says. He pulls off my shoes and socks and begins rubbing my feet, and I swear to God I moan because it's heavenly. I don't think anyone has ever rubbed my feet. His expert fingers work their way up and down my calves and over the arches and balls of my feet.

"How was your night?" His voice is quiet.

"Long. I had a party that wanted to stay until sunup. It was all I could do to get them out of there. I'm so tired. How was my dad?"

"Good. He's still tired. He's been through a lot. We ate dinner and watched a few shoot 'em ups. When he started drifting off in his chair, I suggested he go to bed. I helped him get ready and tucked him in. I checked on him a little bit ago, and he was lightly snoring. I did such a good job; I should add elderly assistant to my resume." He looks so proud, and a zap of relief goes right through me.

"There is somewhere I want to take you and your dad tomorrow. Do you have time before work?"

"Sure. I was just going to hang out with him. Do you think he's up for it?"

"It won't be a lot. Probably be nice for him to get some fresh air. I'll drive through Arby's for lunch, and we'll take it with us. If he isn't doing well in the morning, or seems too tired, we can go another day."

"Okay, that sounds good."

THE NEXT MORNING COMES, and I wake to the smell of bacon cooking. I leap out of bed, forgetting Ferris slept next to me all night. In my mind, my dad is out there about to burn the place down. I come to a complete halt when I spot my dad already dressed, sitting in his recliner with a cup of coffee next to him, and Ferris at the stove with a spatula in his hand, big smile plastered on his face.

My shoulders sag, and I sigh in relief. It doesn't take long for my fear to turn the corner to contentment. What a perfect sight. My two favorite men in one room. One cooking and one just... living. How did I get so lucky?

"Come here." Ferris waves me over, and I shuffle over and curl into his side. He kisses my hair. "Sorry, I thought we were being quiet. Although, just a side note, getting your dad dressed for the day is never a quiet process. I'm surprised you didn't hear us."

"I didn't hear you at all. I smelled the bacon and thought it was Dad trying to cook."

His chuckle is deep and hardy and causes warmth to spread from my heart to my toes. "Nope, your kitchen is safe with me. Now go get dressed. We'll eat breakfast and go on our little adventure. I figure your dad is good right now, but as the day goes on, he'll get tired. We can drive thru Arby's on the way home."

Whatever his plans are, he's excited, so I tip my chin up for a quick smooch and head into my room to get ready for the day.

An hour later Ferris is driving, my dad is riding shotgun, and I'm in the middle back seat leaned forward as we turn onto the dirt road leading to Pax and Shay's house. We've been here before so I can't imagine why he's so excited about it. Instead of making the turn toward their house though, he keeps going straight. At last, he turns between two fence posts and drives down a winding dirt road. At the end, I spot a house, probably built in the 1960's, but kept up nicely. The outside walls are large river rock you don't see in modern construction, but something I always thought gave nice character to the homes. There's a medium sized wooden front porch with a broken-down swing and an old rocking chair on it. We come to a stop. As I'm surveying the house, a big, white, expensive SUV pulls up next to us and an overly made up, very professional woman with hair coiffed to perfection climbs out.

"Come on, you guys. Let's go look inside," Ferris says and climbs out of the car. "Hello, Ronnie. Thanks for meeting us on such short notice."

"No problem," she croons at him, and I instantly bristle. She needs to not smile so brightly at my man. I help my dad out of the car as Ferris grabs his walker and converses with

Ronnie. I stay quiet, afraid I might claw her eyes out as I wait for Ferris to elaborate. After we get my dad up the couple of steps and inside, I realize whoever owned this house updated the inside completely. All new appliances, flooring, and even new ceiling fans. It's beautiful.

Ronnie begins to ramble off the stats of the home. "Built in 1962. Updated two years ago, new roof three years ago, on five acres with the option to buy the adjoining five next door. Three bedrooms, two baths, screened in back porch. There is a barn on the back of the property that needs a little love and care but not too much."

We're wandering around the place, checking it all out, when I hear her refer to the barn. I stop and look up to find Ferris smiling at me.

"A barn?" a whisper, afraid I heard her wrong.

"Yeah, it has a barn. Let's go see it. Ronnie, can you keep an eye on Paul for a couple of minutes. We're going to walk back there. I think that's too far for him to walk."

"Um... sure." Ronnie glances at Paul uneasily, but he's put her on the spot so she can't say no.

"We'll make it quick. Come on." He opens the back door and about fifty yards back from the house is a medium-sized faded brown barn. When we approach, he grabs my hand and squeezes. "What do you think so far?"

"It's beautiful, but it's a lot of room for a single guy who doesn't even know if he's going to be here next month."

He stops walking and stares at me for a second with his head tilted. "I'm not single," is his odd reply.

"Well, you're not married."

"No, but I want to be." It's my turn to tilt my head in question. "Don't worry I'm not popping the question...yet. But I'm not single, and yes, I do know I'll be here in a month. I took a job at Sunset Security this week. I also know that with a little work this barn could hold some horses. I also know my girlfriend would love to own one, rent out space, and care for horses for a living."

"I can't quit my job to work in the stable. That was a dream, not reality."

"Why not? I want you and your dad to move in with me, into this house. Help me fix up this barn and take in some horses to care for them. Gigi could just as easily drive here to spend time with your dad while you work out here. Then she's not out late at night, and you're doing what you love."

I stand there staring at him with my mouth hanging open. There is no way it's possible he's about to make most of my dreams come true, standing outside in the brutal Florida heat, while I'm certain Ronnie, the overdone realtor, peeks at us out the window. It all seems too crazy.

"Are you for real?"

"Yep." His lips tip higher as he moves in closer to me and tilts my chin up to his. "I'm for real, and I'm crazy about you. It's time we accept the good coming our way, together. Your dad and I get along well, and I don't mind helping out with him. It can all work out if you believe we have a future together. I do." He eyes me expentantly.

I close my eyes for a second as I fight the urge to question this and say no or even maybe. I mean we haven't known each other that long. It's nuts. My heart tries to take over. Don't do this. Don't turn down the best offer of your life from the best man you've ever met. When I open my eyes, he must see the resolution in them because he grabs me around the waist, hoists me in the air and spins me around like a lunatic laughing and shouting. When he finally sets me down, a tear of happiness slides out of my eye and down my face.

"Never again, my sweet girl. No more tears. We have a happy life to live."

I wrap my arms around my cocky, sweet, nerdy, amazing veteran, and thank God for the day he sat in my section at work.

COCKY HERO CLUB

Want to keep up with all of the new releases in Vi Keeland and Penelope Ward's Cocky Hero Club world? Make sure you sign up for the official Cocky Hero Club newsletter for all the latest on our upcoming books:
https://www.subscribepage.com/CockyHeroClub

Check out other books in the Cocky Hero Club series:
http://www.cockyheroclub.com

ACKNOWLEDGMENTS

Work on this story came during a time of crazy transition in my life so it took longer than I planned. I need to give a special thank you to Teddy, Mykenzie, Tristen, Cassidy, Kat Mizera, Judy King, and Judy Swinson for encouraging me to keep writing. You all know how much I love writing and how badly I just needed to push through. You guys are the best cheerleaders and coaches.

Much appreciation to Vi Keeland, Penelope Ward, and the Cocky Hero team! Thank you for the opportunity to write in the Cocky Hero world and for having patience with the pace of my process.

The biggest thanks goes to Toni Kay Armstrong Treadway for loaning me your name and little life details to use in the story. Although this is a work of fiction it was fun to use some real names, one of those being a huge fan of romance novels. Readers like you are what make this industry so much fun!

Heather Finley, your Eagle-Eye saved me and Katie MacGregor your support and assistance mean so much! I couldn't do it without you ladies!

To my TLC crew...What you find is what you find! As you know these are important words to live by. I love you all and the constant support you've given me in our seventeen years of friendship and the last six years of writing.

And last, but not least, a huge thank you to my readers.

A million thank yous for picking up my books and giving me a chance, especially those who keep coming back. You guys will love what I have lined up next!

ABOUT THE AUTHOR

The west coast of Florida is home for Tiffani and her family. She's a music loving, baseball adoring, crazed hockey fan who enjoys writing sexy romance novels and volunteering in her community.

To learn more about Tiffani Lynn visit:
https://www.tiffanilynn.com

Made in the USA
Columbia, SC
23 February 2024

31947477R00115